W9-DHJ-649

by Herbert Goldstone
What happens when a robot learns to play
the piano?

THE EXACT SCIENCE OF MATRIMONY
by O. Henry
A true con man doesn't know when to stop.

THE WILD DUCK'S NEST
by Michael McLaverty
A wild duck and a young boy make a
strange marriage.

THREE LETTERS . . . AND A FOOTNOTE
by Horacio Quiroga
New light on the old game of "footsie."

THE WIFE
by Washington Irving
The greatest pleasures of matrimony aren't
always those that first meet the eye.

I SEE YOU NEVER
by Ray Bradbury
A new twist from the great science-fiction writer.

THE PHŒNIX
by Sylvia Townsend Warner
Rebirth can be a pretty deadly business.

THE WORLD'S BEST
SHORT SHORT STORIES

A NEW COLLECTION OF FAST-PACED SHORTIES
FOR READERS WHO CAN'T WAIT
TO GET TO THE END

THE WORLD'S BEST SHORT SHORT STORIES

Edited by Roger B. Goodman

BANTAM  BOOKS

BANTAM PATHFINDER EDITIONS
NEW YORK / TORONTO / LONDON

RLI: VLM 7.0
IL 7.12

THE WORLD'S BEST SHORT SHORT STORIES
A Bantam Pathfinder edition / published May 1967
5 printings through August 1972
6th printing
7th printing

ACKNOWLEDGMENTS

"A Wedding without Musicians" by Sholom Aleichem. Reprinted from Tevye's Daughters by Sholom Aleichem. © 1949 by the children of Sholom Aleichem and Crown Publishers, Inc.

"Señor Payroll" by William E. Barrett. Originally published in SOUTHWEST REVIEW, reprinted by permission of Harold Ober Associates Inc. Copyright 1943 by Southwest Review.

"I See You Never" by Ray Bradbury. Copyright 1947 by Ray Bradbury. Originally appeared in THE NEW YORKER, reprinted by permission of The Harold Matson Company, Inc.

"Luck" by Samuel Clemens. Reprinted from The American Claimant and Other Stories by Samuel L. Clemens, by permission of Harper & Brothers.

"The Test" by Angelica Gibbs. Reprinted by permission from THE NEW YORKER. Copyright © 1940 The New Yorker Magazine, Inc.

"Virtuoso" by Herbert Goldstone. © 1953 by Mercury Press Inc. Reprinted from THE MAGAZINE OF FANTASY AND SCIENCE FICTION.

"The Exact Science of Matrimony" from The Gentle Grafter, by O. Henry. Copyright 1907 by Doubleday & Company, Inc. Reprinted by permission of the publisher.

"The Wild Duck's Nest" from The Game Cock and Other Stories by Michael McLaverty. Published 1947 by The Devin-Adair Company; copyright 1947 by The Devin-Adair Company. Reprinted by permission of the publisher. Also reprinted by permission of Michael McLaverty and Jonathan Cape Limited.

"The Standard of Living" from The Portable Dorothy Parker by Dorothy Parker. Originally published in THE NEW YORKER. Copyright 1941 by Dorothy Parker. Reprinted by permission of The Viking Press, Inc.

"Three Letters . . . and a Footnote" by Horacio Quiroga. Reprinted by permission of Crown Publishers, Inc. from A World of Great Stories edited by Hiram Haydn and John Couros. © 1947 by Crown Publishers, Inc. Used by permission of Crown Publishers, Inc.

"The Three Hermits" by Leo Tolstoy. Reprinted from Twenty-Three Tales, World's Classics Series, by Leo Tolstoy, translated by Louise and Aylmer Maude, by permission of The Oxford University Press.

"The Phœnix" from The Cat's Cradle Book by Sylvia Townsend Warner. Copyright 1940 by Sylvia Townsend Warner. Reprinted by permission of The Viking Press, Inc.

"The Hour of Letdown" from The Second Tree from the Corner by E. B. White. Copyright 1951 by E. B. White. Originally appeared in THE NEW YORKER, and reprinted by permission of Harper & Row, Publishers.

Bantam Books are published by Bantam Books, Inc., a National General company. Its trade-mark, consisting of the words "Bantam Books" and the portrayal of a bantam, is registered in the United States Patent Office and in other countries. Marca Registrada. Bantam Books, Inc., 666 Fifth Avenue, New York, N.Y. 10019.

PRINTED IN THE UNITED STATES OF AMERICA

Contents

Preface

The short-story writer is like a fisherman pursuing an extremely wary trout. In order to hook his game he must be poised and ready and skillful. The trout, of course, is his reader—who must be lured, baited and hooked. The very first thing in the writer's kit of lures is the title, which must whet the reader's appetite—or he will, like some bored old fish, nose the bait aside and move on. But, unlike the fisherman, the writer must do more than simply catch his reader's attention: he must hold it and also entertain the reader in doing so. Because the writer is often writing of people, places and events which are unhappy, unpleasant or ugly, his is a most difficult task.

But the short story is a very rich literary form. No human thought or feeling, no subject—no matter how familiar or how strange and exotic—no life is foreign to it. It is the writer's talent to strike sharply and directly at the heart of all the problems of human life, because his is the eye which sees freshly and deeply, the hand which paints meaningfully and beautifully. Even when staring into the face of war, hatred, bias, or degradation, the reader is engaged by his vision, hooked by the image of life the writer creates and hopefully, enriched by the experience of the life and art of which he has been a part.

Though defining the short story precisely is probably impossible because of its richness and variety—some critics ironically have said that a short story is simply a story that is short—its general outlines are clear. While the novel shows us the landscape of a society and the myriad and various human beings who people it, the short story usually limits itself to a few characters, rarely more than three. While the novel generally covers long periods of time and many events in its characters' lives, showing them growing, developing and changing, while rendering them to us in depth and detail, the short story is almost always like a chink in the wall of character and event—a flashing light on the landscape of the human heart—where one glimpses swiftly and glancingly some turning point in a single human life. To the degree that the reader laughs or cries at what he sees and hears, feels horror or delight or relief or chagrin, to the degree that he sympathizes and understands, to that degree has the writer been successful and the reader served.

ROGER B. GOODMAN

A Wedding without Musicians

BY SHOLOM ALEICHEM

The last time I told you about our Straggler Special, I described the miracle of *Hashono Rabo*. This time I shall tell you about another miracle in which the Straggler Special figured, how thanks to the Straggler Special the town of Heissin was saved from a terrible fate.

This took place during the days of the Constitution when reprisals against the Jews were going on everywhere. Though I must tell you that we Jews of Heissin have never been afraid of pogroms. Why? Simply because there is no one in our town who can carry out a pogrom. Of course you can imagine that if we looked very hard we could find one or two volunteers who wouldn't deny themselves the pleasure of ventilating us a little, that is, breaking our bones or burning down our houses. For example, when reports of pogroms began drifting in, the few squires, who are enemies of our people, wrote confidential letters to the proper authorities, saying it might be a good idea if "something were done" in Heissin also; but since there was no one here to do it, would they be so kind as to send help, in other words, would they dispatch some "people" as quickly as possible.

And before another twenty-four hours had passed a reply came, also confidentially, that "people" were being sent. From where? From Zhmerinko, from Kazatin, Razdilno, Popelno and other such places that had distinguished themselves in beating up Jews. Do you

3

want to know how we learned of this deep secret? We found it out through our regular source of news, Noah Tonkonoy. Noah Tonkonoy is a man whom God has endowed with a pair of extra-long legs and he uses them to good purpose. He never rests and he is seldom to be found at home. He is always busy with a thousand things and most of these things have to do with other people's business rather than his own. By trade he is a printer, and because he is the only printer in Heissin he knows all the squires and the police and has dealings with officialdom and is in on all their secrets.

Noah Tonkonoy spread the good news all over town. He told the secret to one person at a time, in strictest confidence, of course, saying, "I am telling this only to you. I wouldn't tell it to anyone else." And that was how the whole town became aware of the fact that a mob of hooligans was on the way, and that a plan for beating up Jews had been worked out. The plan told exactly when they would start, on which day, at which hour, and from which point, and by what means—everything to the last detail.

You can imagine what terror this struck in our hearts. Panic spread quickly. And among whom do you think it spread first? Among the poor, of course. It's a peculiar thing about poor people. When a rich man is afraid of a pogrom, you can understand why. He is afraid, poor fellow, that he will be turned into a pauper. But those of you who are already paupers, what are you afraid of? What have you got to lose? But you should have seen how they bundled up their children and packed up their belongings and began running hither and yon, looking for a place to hide. Where can a person hide? This one hides in a friendly peasant's cellar, another in the Notary's attic, a third in the Director's office at the factory. Everyone finds a spot for himself.

I was the only one in town who wasn't anxious to hide. I am not boasting about my bravery. But this is the way I see it: what's the sense of being afraid of a

pogrom? I don't say that I am a hero. I might have
been willing to hide too, when the hour of reckoning
came. But I asked myself first, "How can I be sure that
during the slaughter the friendly peasant in whose
cellar I was hiding, or the Notary, or the Director of
the factory himself, wouldn't . . ." You understand.
And all that aside, how can you leave a town wide
open like that? It's no trick to run away. You have to
see about doing something. But, alas, what can a Jew
do? He appeals to a friendly official. And that is just
what we did.

In every town there is at least one friendly official
you can appeal to. We had one too, the Inspector of
Police, a jewel of a fellow, willing to listen to us and
willing to accept a gift on occasion. We went to the Inspector with the proper gifts and asked for his protection. He reassured us at once. He told us to go home
and sleep in peace. Nothing would happen. Sounds
good, doesn't it? But we still had our walking newspaper, Noah, who was broadcasting another secret
through the length and breadth of the town. The secret
was that a telegram had just arrived. He swore by everything holy that he had seen it himself. What was in that
telegram? Only one word—*Yediem*. An ugly word. It
means simply, "We are coming." We ran back to the
Inspector. "Your honor," we told him, "it looks bad."
"What looks bad?" he asked, and we told him, "A
telegram has just arrived." "From where?" We told
him. "And what does it say?" We told him, *"Yediem."*
At this he burst out laughing. "You are big fools," he
said. "Only yesterday I ordered a regiment of Cossacks
from Tolchin."

When we heard this we breathed more easily. When
a Jew hears that a Cossack is coming, he takes courage,
he can face the world again. The question remained:
who would arrive first, the Cossacks from Tolchin, or
the hooligans from Zhmerinko? Common sense told us
that the hooligans would arrive first, because they were
coming by train, while the Cossacks were coming on

horseback. But we pinned all our hopes on the Straggler Special. God is merciful. He would surely perform a miracle and the Straggler would be at least a few hours late. This wasn't too much to hope for, since it happened nearly every day. But this one time it looked as though the miracle wouldn't take place. The Straggler kept going from station to station as regular as a clock. You can imagine how we felt when we learned, confidentially, of course, through Noah Tonkonoy, that a telegram had arrived from the last station, from Krishtopovka. *Yediem,* it said, and not just *yediem*—but *yediem* with a *hurrah!* in front of it.

Naturally we took this last bit of news straight to the Inspector. We begged him not to rely on the Cossacks who might or might not arrive from Tolchin sometime, but to send police to the station, at least for the sake of appearances, so that our enemies wouldn't think that we were completely at their mercy. The Inspector listened to our pleas. He did what we asked, and more. He got himself up in full uniform, with all his orders and medals, and took the whole police force, that is the gendarme and his assistant, to the station with him to meet the train.

But our enemies weren't asleep either. They also put on their full dress uniforms, complete with ribbons and medals, took a couple of priests along, and also came to meet the train. The Inspector asked them sternly, "What are you doing here?" And they asked him the same question, "What are you doing here?" They bandied words back and forth, and the Inspector let them know in no uncertain terms that their trouble was for nothing. As long as he was in charge, there would be no pogrom in Heissin. They listened, smiled knowingly, and answered with insolence, "We shall see."

Just then a train whistle was heard from the distance. The sound struck terror to our hearts. We waited for another whistle to blow and after that for the shouts of "Hurrah!" What would happen after the Hurrah! we knew only too well from hearsay. We waited, but heard nothing more. What had happened? The sort of thing that could only happen to our Straggler Special.

When the Straggler Special drew into the station, the engineer stopped the locomotive, stepped out calmly and made his way toward the buffet. We met him halfway. "Well, my good fellow, and where are the cars?" "Which cars?" "Can't you see that you are here with the locomotive and without cars?"

He stared at us. "What do I care about the cars? They are the business of the crew." "Where is the crew?" "How should I know where the crew is? The conductor blows the whistle when he is ready and I whistle back to let him know that I am starting, and off we go. I don't have an extra pair of eyes in back of my head to see what's going on behind me." That was his story and according to that he was right. But right or wrong, there stood the Straggler Special without cars and without passengers. In other words, it was a wedding without musicians.

Later we learned that a band of hooligans had been on the way to Heissin, all of them handpicked youths, armed to the teeth with clubs and knives and other weapons. Their spirits were high and liquor flowed freely. At the last station, Krishtopovka, they invited the crew to join them and treated everybody to drinks —the conductor, the fireman, the gendarmes. But in the midst of this revelry they forgot one little detail, to couple the cars back to the locomotive. And so the locomotive went off at the usual time to Heissin and the rest of the Straggler Special remained standing in Krishtopovka.

Neither the hooligans nor the other passengers on the crew noticed that they were standing still. They continued to empty bottle after bottle and to make merry, until the station master suddenly noticed that the locomotive had gone off and left the cars behind. He spread the alarm, the crew came tumbling out. A hue and cry was raised. The hooligans blamed the crew, the crew blamed the hooligans, but what good did it do? At last they decided that the only thing to do was to set out for Heissin on foot. They took heart and began marching toward Heissin, singing and shouting as they went.

And so they arrived in their usual good form, singing and yelling and brandishing their clubs. But it was already too late. In the streets of Heissin the Cossacks from Tolchin were riding up and down on horseback with whips in their hands. Within half an hour not one of the hooligans remained in town. They ran off like rats in a famine, they melted like ice in summer.

Now, I ask you, didn't the Straggler Special deserve to be showered with gold, or at least written up?

Señor Payroll

BY WILLIAM E. BARRETT

❦ ❦ ❦

Larry and I were Junior Engineers in the gas plant, which means that we were clerks. Anything that could be classified as paper work came to the flat double desk across which we faced each other. The Main Office downtown sent us a bewildering array of orders and rules that were to be put into effect.

Junior Engineers were beneath the notice of everyone except the Mexican laborers at the plant. To them we were the visible form of a distant, unknowable paymaster. We were Señor Payroll.

Those Mexicans were great workmen; the aristocrats among them were the stokers, big men who worked Herculean eight-hour shifts in the fierce heat of the retorts. They scooped coal with huge shovels and hurled it with uncanny aim at tiny doors. The coal streamed out from the shovels like black water from a high-pressure nozzle, and never missed the narrow opening. The stokers worked stripped to the waist, and there was pride and dignity in them. Few men could do such work, and they were the few.

The Company paid its men only twice a month, on the fifth and on the twentieth. To a Mexican, this was absurd. What man with money will make it last fifteen days? If he hoarded money beyond the spending of three days, he was a miser—and when, Señor, did the blood of Spain flow in the veins of misers? Hence, it was the custom for our stokers to appear every third or fourth day to draw the money due to them.

9

There was a certain elasticity in the Company rules, and Larry and I sent the necessary forms to the Main Office and received an "advance" against a man's pay check. Then, one day, Downtown favored us with a memorandum:

"There have been too many abuses of the advance-against-wages privilege. Hereafter, no advance against wages will be made to any employee except in a case of genuine emergency."

We had no sooner posted the notice when in came stoker Juan Garcia. He asked for an advance. I pointed to the notice. He spelled it through slowly, then said, "What does this mean, this 'genuine emergency'?"

I explained to him patiently that the Company was kind and sympathetic, but that it was a great nuisance to have to pay wages every few days. If someone was ill or if money was urgently needed for some other good reason, then the Company would make an exception to the rule.

Juan Garcia turned his hat over and over slowly in his big hands. "I do not get my money?"

"Next payday, Juan. On the twentieth."

He went out silently and I felt a little ashamed of myself. I looked across the desk at Larry. He avoided my eyes.

In the next hour two other stokers came in, looked at the notice, had it explained and walked solemnly out; then no more came. What we did not know was that Juan Garcia, Pete Mendoza, and Francisco Gonzalez had spread the word, and that every Mexican in the plant was explaining the order to every other Mexican. "To get money now, the wife must be sick. There must be medicine for the baby."

The next morning Juan Garcia's wife was practically dying, Pete Mendoza's mother would hardly last the day, there was a veritable epidemic among children, and, just for variety, there was one sick father. We always suspected that the old man was really sick; no Mexican would otherwise have thought of him. At any rate, nobody paid Larry and me to examine private lives; we made out our forms with an added line describing the "genuine emergency." Our people got paid.

That went on for a week. Then came a new order, curt and to the point: "Hereafter, employees will be paid ONLY on the fifth and the twentieth of the month. No exceptions will be made except in the cases of employees leaving the service of the Company."

The notice went up on the board, and we explained its significance gravely. "No, Juan Garcia, we cannot advance your wages. It is too bad about your wife and your cousins and your aunts, but there is a new rule."

Juan Garcia went out and thought it over. He thought out loud with Mendoza and Gonzalez and Ayala, then, in the morning, he was back. "I am quitting this company for different job. You pay me now?"

We argued that it was a good company and that it loved its employees like children, but in the end we paid off, because Juan Garcia quit. And so did Gonzalez Mendoza, Obregon, Ayala and Ortez, the best stokers, men who could not be replaced.

Larry and I looked at each other; we knew what was coming in about three days. One of our duties was to sit on the hiring line early each morning, engaging transient workers for the handy gangs. Any man was accepted who could walk up and ask for a job without falling down. Never before had we been called upon to hire such skilled virtuosos as stokers for handy-gang work, but we were called upon to hire them now.

The day foreman was wringing his hands and asking the Almighty if he was personally supposed to shovel this condemned coal, while there in a stolid, patient line were skilled men—Garcia, Mendoza, and others—waiting to be hired. We hired them, of course. There was nothing else to do.

Every day we had a line of resigning stokers, and another line of stokers seeking work. Our paper work became very complicated. At the Main Office they were jumping up and down. The procession of forms showing Juan Garcia's resigning and being hired over and over again was too much for them. Sometimes Downtown had Garcia on the prayroll twice at the same time when someone down there was slow in entering a resignation. Our phone rang early and often.

Tolerantly and patiently we explained: "There's nothing we can do if a man wants to quit, and if there are stokers available when the plant needs stokers, we hire them."

Out of chaos, Downtown issued another order. I read it and whistled. Larry looked at it and said, "It is going to be very quiet around here."

The order read: "Hereafter, no employee who resigns may be rehired within a period of 30 days."

Juan Garcia was due for another resignation, and when he came in we showed him the order and explained that standing in line the next day would do him no good if he resigned today. "Thirty days is a long time, Juan."

It was a grave matter and he took time to reflect on it. So did Gonzalez, Mendoza, Ayala and Ortez. Ultimately, however, they were all back—and all resigned.

We did our best to dissuade them and we were sad about the parting. This time it was for keeps and they shook hands with us solemnly. It was very nice knowing us. Larry and I looked at each other when they were gone and we both knew that neither of us had been pulling for Downtown to win this duel. It was a blue day.

In the morning, however, they were all back in line. With the utmost gravity, Juan Garcia informed me that he was a stoker looking for a job.

"No dice, Juan," I said. "Come back in thirty days. I warned you."

His eyes looked straight into mine without a flicker. "There is some mistake, Señor," he said. "I am Manuel Hernandez. I work as the stoker in Pueblo, in Santa Fe, in many places."

I stared back at him, remembering the sick wife and the babies without medicine, the mother-in-law in the hospital, the many resignations and the rehirings. I knew that there was a gas plant in Pueblo, and that there wasn't any in Santa Fe; but who was I to argue with a man about his own name? A stoker is a stoker.

So I hired him. I hired Gonzalez, too, who swore that his name was Carrera and Ayala, who had shamelessly become Smith.

Three days later the resigning started.

Within a week our payroll read like a history of Latin America. Everyone was on it: Lopez and Obregon, Villa, Diaz, Batista, Gomez, and even San Martín and Bolívar. Finally Larry and I, growing weary of staring at familiar faces and writing unfamiliar names, went to the Superintendent and told him the whole story. He tried not to grin, and said, "Damned nonsense!"

The next day the orders were taken down. We called our most prominent stokers into the office and pointed to the board. No rules any more.

"The next time we hire you hombres," Larry said grimly, "come in under the names you like best, because that's the way you are going to stay on the books."

They looked at us and they looked at the board; then for the first time in the long duel, their teeth flashed white. "Si, Señores," they said.

And so it was.

How Light Belief Bringeth Damage

BY BIDPAI

Two skillful thieves one night entered the house of a wealthy knight, no less wise than worshipped in the community. The gentleman, hearing the noise of their feet in the house, awakened and suspected that they were thieves. They were upon the point of opening the door of the chamber wherein he lay, when he jogged his wife, awakened her, and whispered, "I hear the noise of thieves who have come to rob us. I would have you, therefore, ask me straight, and with great insistence, whence and by what means I came by all I own. Ask me loudly and earnestly, and, as I shall appear reluctant, you must plead and wheedle until, at length, I shall succumb and tell you." The Lady, his wife, being wise and subtle, began in this manner to question her husband—"O, dear sir. Grant me one thing this night that I have for so long desired to know. Tell me how you have come by all these goods you now possess." He, speaking at random and carelessly, scarce answered. Finally, after she kept pleading, he said, "I can but wonder, Madam, at what moves you to know my secrets. Be contented, then, to live well, to dress richly, and to be waited upon and served. I have heard that all things have ears, and that many things are spoken which are later repented. Therefore, I pray you, hold your peace."

But even this did not deter the Lady. Sweetly and lovingly enticing, she besought him to tell her. Finally, wearying of her speech, the knight said, "All we have—

14

and I charge you to say nothing of this to anyone—
is stolen. Indeed, of all I own I got nothing truly." The
Lady, unbelieving, so berated her husband that he answered farther, "You think what I have already told
you is a wonder. Listen then. Even in my cradle I delighted in stealing and filching. And I lived among
thieves so that my fingers might never be idle. One
friend among them loved me so well that he taught me
a rare and singular trick. He taught me a conjuration which I made to the moonbeams—enabling me
to embrace them suddenly. Thus I sometimes came
down upon them from a high window—or served myself
with them to go up again to the top of the house. So
I used them as I would. The Moon, hearing my conjuration seven times, showed me all the money and treasure
of the house and with her beams I flew up and down.
And thus, good wife, I made me rich. Now, no more."

One of the thieves, listening at the door, heard all
that was said and bore it away. Because the knight
was known to be a man of credit and integrity, the
thieves believed his story. The chief thief, desirous to
prove in deeds what he had heard in words, repeated
the conjuration seven times, and then, embracing the
moonbeams, he cast himself upon them thinking to go
from window to window, and he fell headlong to the
ground. The moon, however, favored him so that he
was not killed, but broke his legs and one arm. He
cried aloud in his pain and at his stupidity in trusting
too much to another's words.

So, lying on the ground expecting death, he was
found by the knight who beat him sorely. The thief
begged for mercy, saying that what hurt him most was
that he was such a fool to believe such words. And he
besought him, since he had hurt him so with words,
he would not also hurt him in deeds.

A Psychological Shipwreck

BY AMBROSE BIERCE

⌘ ⌘ ⌘

In the summer of 1874 I was in Liverpool, whither
I had gone on business for the mercantile house of
Bronson & Jarrett, New York. I am William Jarrett;
my partner was Zenas Bronson. The firm failed last
year, and unable to endure the fall from affluence to
poverty he died.

Having finished my business, and feeling the las-
situde and exhaustion incident to its dispatch, I felt
that a protracted sea voyage would be both agreeable
and beneficial, so instead of embarking for my return
on one of the many fine passenger steamers I booked
for New York on the sailing vessel *Morrow*, upon
which I had shipped a large and valuable invoice of
the goods I had bought. The *Morrow* was an English
ship with, of course, but little accommodation for passengers, of whom there were only myself, a young
woman and her servant, who was a middle-aged
Negress. I thought it singular that a traveling English
girl should be so attended, but she afterward explained
to me that the woman had been left with her family
by a man and his wife from South Carolina, both of
whom had died on the same day at the house of the
young lady's father in Devonshire—a circumstance in
itself sufficiently uncommon to remain rather distinctly
in my memory, even had it not afterward transpired in
conversation with the young lady that the name of the
man was William Jarrett, the same as my own. I knew

that a branch of my family had settled in South Carolina, but of them and their history I was ignorant.

The *Morrow* sailed from the mouth of the Mersey on the 15th of June and for several weeks we had fair breezes and unclouded skies. The skipper, an admirable seaman but nothing more, favored us with very little of his society, except at his table; and the young woman, Miss Janette Harford, and I became very well acquainted. We were, in truth, nearly always together, and being of an introspective turn of mind I often endeavored to analyze and define the novel feeling with which she inspired me—a secret, subtle, but powerful attraction which constantly impelled me to seek her; but the attempt was hopeless. I could only be sure that at least it was not love. Having assured myself of this and being certain that she was quite as whole-hearted, I ventured one evening (I remember it was on the 3rd of July) as we sat on deck to ask her, laughingly, if she could assist me to resolve my psychological doubt.

For a moment she was silent, with averted face, and I began to fear I had been extremely rude and indelicate; then she fixed her eyes gravely on my own. In an instant my mind was dominated by as strange a fancy as ever entered human consciousness. It seemed as if she were looking at me, not *with,* but *through,* those eyes—from an immeasurable distance behind them—and that a number of other persons, men, women and children, upon whose faces I caught strangely familiar evanescent expressions, clustered about her, struggling with gentle eagerness to look at me through the same orbs. Ship, ocean, sky—all had vanished. I was conscious of nothing but the figures in this extraordinary and fantastic scene. Then all at once darkness fell upon me, and anon from out of it, as to one who grows accustomed by degrees to a dimmer light, my former surroundings of deck and mast and cordage slowly resolved themselves. Miss Harford had closed her eyes and was leaning back in her chair, apparently asleep, the book she had been reading open in her lap. Impelled by surely I cannot say what motive, I glanced at the top of the page; it was a copy of that rare and curious work, "Denneker's Meditations," and the lady's index finger rested on this passage:

"To sundry it is given to be drawn away, and to be apart from the body for a season; for, as concerning rills which would flow across each other the weaker is borne along by the stronger, so there be certain of kin whose paths intersecting, their souls do bear company, the while their bodies go fore-appointed ways, unknowing."

Miss Harford arose, shuddering; the sun had sunk below the horizon, but it was not cold. There was not a breath of wind; there were no clouds in the sky, yet not a star was visible. A hurried tramping sounded on the deck; the captain, summoned from below, joined the first officer, who stood looking at the barometer. "Good God!" I heard him exclaim.

An hour later the form of Janette Harford, invisible in the darkness and spray, was torn from my grasp by the cruel vortex of the sinking ship, and I fainted in the cordage of the floating mast to which I had lashed myself.

It was by lamplight that I awoke. I lay in a berth amid the familiar surroundings of the stateroom of a steamer. On a couch opposite sat a man, half undressed for bed, reading a book. I recognized the face of my friend Gordon Doyle, whom I had met in Liverpool on the day of my embarkation, when he was himself about to sail on the steamer *City of Prague,* on which he had urged me to accompany him.

After some moments I now spoke his name. He simply said, "Well," and turned a leaf in his book without removing his eyes from the page.

"Doyle," I repeated, "did they save *her?*"

He now deigned to look at me and smiled as if amused. He evidently thought me but half awake.

"Her? Whom do you mean?"

"Janette Harford."

His amusement turned to amazement; he stared at me fixedly, saying nothing.

"You will tell me after a while," I continued; "I suppose you will tell me after a while."

A moment later I asked: "What ship is this?"

Doyle stared again. "The steamer *City of Prague*, bound from Liverpool to New York, three weeks out with a broken shaft. Principal passenger, Mr. Gordon Doyle; ditto lunatic, Mr. William Jarrett. These two distinguished travelers embarked together, but they are about to part, it being the resolute intention of the former to pitch the latter overboard."

I sat bolt upright. "Do you mean to say that I have been for three weeks a passenger on this steamer?"

"Yes, pretty nearly; this is the 3d of July."

"Have I been ill?"

"Right as a trivet all the time, and punctual at your meals."

"My God! Doyle, there is some mystery here; do have the goodness to be serious. Was I not rescued from the wreck of the ship *Morrow?*"

Doyle changed color, and approaching me, laid his fingers on my wrist. A moment later, "What do you know of Janette Harford?" he asked very calmly.

"First tell me what *you* know of her?"

Mr. Doyle gazed at me for some moments as if thinking what to do, then seating himself again on the couch, said:

"Why should I not? I am engaged to marry Janette Harford, whom I met a year ago in London. Her family, one of the wealthiest in Devonshire, cut up rough about it, and we eloped—are eloping rather, for on the day that you and I walked to the landing stage to go aboard this steamer she and her faithful servant, a Negress, passed us, driving to the ship *Morrow*. She would not consent to go in the same vessel with me, and it had been deemed best that she take a sailing vessel in order to avoid observation and lessen the risk of detection. I am now alarmed lest this cursed breaking of our machinery may detain us so long that the *Morrow* will get to New York before us, and the poor girl will not know where to go."

I lay still in my berth—so still I hardly breathed. But the subject was evidently not displeasing to Doyle, and after a short pause he resumed:

"By the way, she is only an adopted daughter of the Harfords. Her mother was killed at their place by being thrown from a horse while hunting, and her father, mad with grief, made away with himself the same day. No one ever claimed the child, and after a reasonable time they adopted her. She was grown up in the belief that she is their daughter."

"Doyle, what book are you reading?"

"Oh, it's called 'Denneker's Meditations.' It's a rum lot, Janette gave it to me; she happened to have two copies. Want to see it?"

He tossed me the volume, which opened as it fell. On one of the exposed pages was a marked passage:

"To sundry it is given to be drawn away, and to be apart from the body for a season; for, as concerning rills which would flow across each other the weaker is borne along by the stronger, so there be certain of kin whose paths intersecting, their souls do bear company, the while their bodies go fore-appointed ways, unknowing."

"She had—she has—a singular taste in reading," I managed to say, mastering my agitation.

"Yes. And now perhaps you will have the kindness to explain how you knew her name and that of the ship she sailed in."

"You talked of her in your sleep," I said.

A week later we were towed into the port of New York. But the *Morrow* was never heard from.

I See You Never

BY RAY BRADBURY

The soft knock came at the kitchen door, and when Mrs. O'Brian opened it, there on the back porch were her best tenant, Mr. Ramirez, and two police officers, one on each side of him. Mr. Ramirez just stood there, walled in and small.

"Why, Mr. Ramirez!" said Mrs. O'Brian.

Mr. Ramirez was overcome. He did not seem to have words to explain.

He had arrived at Mrs. O'Brian's rooming house more than two years earlier and had lived there ever since. He had come by bus from Mexico City to San Diego and had then gone up to Los Angeles. There he had found the clean little room, with glossy blue linoleum, and pictures and calendars on the flowered walls, and Mrs. O'Brian as the strict but kindly landlady. During the war he had worked at the airplane factory and made parts for the planes that flew off somewhere, and even now, after the war, he still held his job. From the first he had made big money. He saved some of it, and he got drunk only once a week—a privilege that to Mrs. O'Brian's way of thinking, every good workingman deserved, unquestioned and unreprimanded.

Inside Mrs. O'Brian's kitchen, pies were baking in the oven. Soon the pies would come out with complexions like Mr. Ramirez'—brown and shiny and crisp, with slits in them for the air almost like the slits of Mr. Ramirez' dark eyes. The kitchen smelled good.

21

The policemen leaned forward, lured by the odor. Mr. Ramirez gazed at his feet, as if they had carried him into all this trouble.

"What happened, Mr. Ramirez?" asked Mrs. O'Brian.

Behind Mrs. O'Brian, as he lifted his eyes, Mr. Ramirez saw the long table laid with clean white linen and set with a platter, cool, shining glasses, and a water pitcher with ice cubes floating inside it, a bowl of fresh potato salad and one of bananas and oranges, cubed and sugared. At this table sat Mrs. O'Brian's children—her three grown sons, eating and conversing, and her two younger daughters, who were staring at the policemen as they ate.

"I have been here thirty months," said Mr. Ramirez quietly, looking at Mrs. O'Brian's plump hands.

"That's six months too long," said one policeman. "He only had a temporary visa. We've just got around to looking for him."

Soon after Mr. Ramirez had arrived he bought a radio for his little room; evenings he turned it up very loud and enjoyed it. And he had bought a wrist watch and enjoyed that too. And on many nights he had walked silent streets and seen the bright clothes in the windows and bought some of them, and he had seen the jewels and bought some of them for his few lady friends. And he had gone to picture shows five nights a week for a while. Then also, he had ridden the street-cars—all night some nights—smelling the electricity, his dark eyes moving over the advertisements, feeling the wheels rumble under him, watching the little sleeping houses and big hotels slip by. Besides that, he had gone to large restaurants, where he had eaten many-course dinners, and to the opera and the theater. And he had bought a car, which later, when he forgot to pay for it, the dealer had driven off angrily from in front of the rooming house.

"So here I am," said Mr. Ramirez now, "to tell you

I must give up my room, Mrs. O'Brian. I come to get my luggage and clothes and go with these men."

"Back to Mexico?"

"Yes. To Lagos. That is a little town north of Mexico City."

"I'm sorry, Mr. Ramirez."

"I'm packed," said Mr. Ramirez hoarsely, blinking his dark eyes rapidly and moving his hands helplessly before him. The policemen did not touch him. There was no necessity for that.

"Here is the key, Mrs. O'Brian," Mr. Ramirez said. "I have my bag already."

Mrs. O'Brian, for the first time, noticed a suitcase standing behind him on the porch.

Mr. Ramirez looked in again at the huge kitchen, at the bright silver cutlery and the young people eating and the shining waxed floor. He turned and looked for a long moment at the apartment house next door, rising up three stories, high and beautiful. He looked at the balconies and fire escapes and back-porch stairs, at the lines of laundry snapping in the wind.

"You've been a good tenant," said Mrs. O'Brian.

"Thank you, thank you, Mrs. O'Brian," he said softly. He closed his eyes.

Mrs. O'Brian stood holding the door half open. One of her sons, behind her, said that her dinner was getting cold, but she shook her head at him and turned back to Mr. Ramirez. She remembered a visit she had once made to some Mexican border towns—the hot days, the endless crickets leaping and falling or lying dead and brittle like the small cigars in the shopwindows, and the canals taking river water out to the farms, the dirt roads, the scorched scape. She remembered the silent towns, the warm beer, the hot, thick foods each day. She remembered the slow, dragging horses and the parched jack rabbits on the road. She remembered the iron mountains and the dusty valleys and the ocean beaches that spread hundreds of miles with no sound but the waves—no cars, no buildings, nothing.

"I'm sure sorry, Mr. Ramirez," she said.

"I don't want to go back, Mrs. O'Brian," he said weakly. "I like it here, I want to stay here. I've worked, I've got money. I look all right, don't I? And I don't want to go back!"

"I'm sorry, Mr. Ramirez," she said. "I wish there was something I could do."

"Mrs. O'Brian!" he cried suddenly, tears rolling out under his eyelids. He reached out his hands and took her hand fervently, shaking it, wringing it, holding to it. "Mrs. O'Brian, I see you never, I see you never!"

The policemen smiled at this. But Mr. Ramirez did not notice it, and they stopped smiling very soon.

"Goodby, Mrs. O'Brian. You have been good to me. Oh, goodby, Mrs. O'Brian. I see you never!"

The policemen waited for Mr. Ramirez to turn, pick up his suitcase, and walk away. Then they followed him, tipping their hats to Mrs. O'Brian. She watched them go down the porch steps. Then she shut the door quietly and went slowly back to her chair at the table. She pulled the chair and sat down. She picked up the shining knife and fork and started once more upon her steak.

"Hurry up, Mom," said one of the sons. "It'll be cold."

Mrs. O'Brian took one bite and chewed on it for a long, slow time; then she stared at the closed door. She laid down her knife and fork.

"What's wrong, Ma?" asked her son.

"I just realized," said Mrs. O'Brian—she put her hand to her face—"I'll never see Mr. Ramirez again."

Luck

BY SAMUEL CLEMENS

It was at a banquet in London in honor of one of the two or three conspicuously illustrious English military names of this generation. For reasons which will presently appear, I will withhold his real name and titles and call him Lieutenant-General Lord Arthur Scoresby, Y.C., K.C.B., etc, etc, etc. What a fascination there is in a renowned name! There sat the man, in actual flesh, whom I had heard of so many thousands of times since that day, thirty years before, when his name shot suddenly to the zenith from a Crimean battlefield, to remain forever celebrated. It was food and drink to me to look, and look, and look at that demigod; scanning, searching, noting: the quietness, the reserve, the noble gravity of his countenance; the simple honesty that expressed itself all over him; the sweet unconsciousness of his greatness—unconsciousness of the hundreds of admiring eyes fastened upon him, unconsciousness of the deep, loving, sincere worship welling out of the breasts of those people and flowing toward him.

The clergyman at my left was an old acquaintance of mine—clergyman now, but had spent the first half of his life in the camp and field and as an instructor in the military school at Woolwich. Just at the moment I have been talking about a veiled and singular light glimmered in his eyes and he leaned down and muttered confidentially to me—indicating the hero of the banquet with a gesture:

25

"Privately—he's an absolute fool."

This verdict was a great surprise to me. If its subject had been Napoleon, or Socrates, or Solomon, my astonishment could not have been greater. Two things I was well aware of: that the Reverend was a man of strict veracity and that his judgment of men was good. Therefore I knew, beyond doubt or question, that the world was mistaken about this hero: he *was* a fool. So I meant to find out, at a convenient moment, how the Reverend, all solitary and alone, had discovered the secret.

Some days later the opportunity came, and this is what the Reverend told me:

About forty years ago I was an instructor in the military academy at Woolwich. I was present in one of the sections when young Scoresby underwent his preliminary examination. I was touched to the quick with pity, for the rest of the class answered up brightly and handsomely, while he—why, dear me, he didn't know anything, so to speak. He was evidently good, and sweet, and lovable, and guileless; and so it was exceedingly painful to see him stand there, as serene as a graven image, and deliver himself of answers which were verily miraculous for stupidity and ignorance. All the compassion in me was aroused in his behalf. I said to myself, when he comes to be examined again he will be flung over, of course; so it will be simply a harmless act of charity to ease his fall as much as I can. I took him aside and found that he knew a little of Caesar's history; and as he didn't know anything else, I went to work and drilled him like a galley-slave on a certain line of stock questions concerning Caesar which I knew would be used. If you'll believe me, he went through with flying colors on examination day! He went through on that purely superficial "cram," and got compliments too, while others, who knew a thousand times more than he, got plucked. By some strangely lucky accident—an accident not likely to happen twice in a century—he was asked no question outside of the narrow limits of his drill.

It was stupefying. Well, all through his course I stood by him, with something of the sentiment which a mother feels for a crippled child; and he always saved himself, just by miracle apparently.

Now, of course, the thing that would expose him and kill him at last was mathematics. I resolved to make his death as easy as I could; so I drilled him and crammed him, and crammed him and drilled him, just on the line of questions which the examiners would be most likely to use, and then launched him on his fate. Well, sir, try to conceive of the result: to my consternation, he took the first prize! And with it he got a perfect ovation in the way of compliments.

Sleep? There was no more sleep for me for a week. My conscience tortured me day and night. What I had done I had done purely through charity, and only to ease the poor youth's fall. I never had dreamed of any such preposterous results as the thing that had happened. I felt as guilty and miserable as Franken-stein. Here was a wooden-head whom I had put in the way of glittering promotions and prodigious responsi-bilities, and but one thing could happen: he and his responsibilities would all go to ruin together at the first opportunity.

The Crimean War had just broken out. Of course there had to be a war, I say to myself. We could have peace and give this donkey a chance to die be-fore he is found out. I waited for the earthquake. It came. And it made me reel when it did come. He was actually gazetted to a captaincy in a marching regi-ment! Better men grow old and gray in the service before they climb to a sublimity like that. And who could ever have foreseen that they would go and put such a load of responsibility on such green and inade-quate shoulders? I could just barely have stood it if they had made him a cornet; but a captain—think of it! I thought my hair would turn white.

Consider what I did—I who so loved repose and inaction. I said to myself, I am responsible to the country for this, and I must go along with him and protect the country against him as far as I can. So I took my poor little capital and went with a sigh and bought a cornetcy in his regiment, and away we went to the field.

And there—oh, dear, it was awful. Blunders?—why, he never did anything *but* blunder. But, you see, nobody was in the fellow's secret. Everybody had him focused wrong, and necessarily misinterpreted his performance every time. Consequently they took his idiotic blunders for inspirations of genius. They did, honestly! His mildest blunders were enough to make a man in his right mind cry; and they did make me cry—and rage and rave, too, privately. And the thing that kept me always in a sweat of apprehension was the fact that every fresh blunder he made always increased the luster of his reputation! I kept saying to myself, he'll get so high that when discovery does finally come it will be like the sun falling out of the sky.

He went right along up, from grade to grade, over the dead bodies of his superiors, until at last, in the hottest moment of the battle of —— down went our colonel, and my heart jumped into my mouth, for Scoresby was next in rank! Now for it, said I; we'll all land in Sheol in ten minutes, sure.

The battle was awfully hot; the allies were steadily giving way all over the field. Our regiment occupied a position that was vital; a blunder now must be destruction. At this crucial moment, what does this immortal fool do but detach the regiment from its place and order a charge over a neighboring hill where there wasn't a suggestion of an enemy! "There you go!" I said to myself; "this *is* the end at last."

And away we did go, and were over the shoulder of the hill before the insane movement could be discovered and stopped. And what did we find? An entire and unsuspected Russian army in reserve! And what happened? We were eaten up? That is necessarily what would have happened in ninety-nine cases out of a hundred. But no; those Russians argued that no single regiment would come browsing around there at such a time. It must be the entire English army, and that the sly Russian game was detected and blocked; so they turned tail, and away they went, pellmell, over the hill and down into the field, in wild confusion, and we after them; they themselves broke the solid Russian center in the field, and tore through, and in no time there was the most tremendous rout you ever saw, and the defeat of the allies was turned into a sweeping and splendid victory! Marshal Canrobert looked on, dizzy with astonishment, admiration, and delight; and sent right off for Scoresby, and hugged him, and decorated him on the field in presence of all the armies!

And what was Scoresby's blunder that time? Merely the mistaking his right hand for his left—that was all. An order had come to him to fall back and support our right; and instead, he fell *forward* and went over the hill to the left. But the name he won that day as a marvelous military genius filled the world with his glory, and that glory will never fade while history books last.

He is just as good and sweet and lovable and unpretending as a man can be, but he doesn't know enough to come in when it rains. Now that is absolutely true. He is the supremest ass in the universe; and until half an hour ago nobody knew it but himself and me. He has been pursued, day by day and year by year, by a most phenomenal and astonishing luckiness. He has been a shining soldier in all our wars for a generation; he has littered his whole military life with blunders, and yet has never committed one that didn't make him a knight or a baronet or a lord or something. Look at his breast; why, he is just clothed in domestic and foreign decorations. Well, sir, every one of them is the record of some shouting stupidity or other; and, taken together, they are proof that the very best thing in all this world that can befall a man is to be born lucky. I say again, as I said at the banquet, Scoresby's an absolute fool.

A Game of Billiards

BY ALPHONSE DAUDET

🙚 🙚 🙚

Even veterans are exhausted after two days' fighting, especially if they have passed the night, knapsacks on their backs, standing in torrents of rain. Yet for three mortal hours they had been left to wait in puddles along the highway; in the mire of rain-soaked fields.

Heavy with fatigue, weakened by the effects of previous nights, their uniforms drenched, they press together for warmth and support. Here and there, leaning upon a comrade's knapsack, a man falls asleep —standing; and upon the relaxed faces of these men, overcome by sleep, may be read more plainly than before the traces which weariness and privation have made. In the mud and rain, without fire, without food; overhead the sky heavy and lowering—around them, on every side, the enemy.

Their cannon, mouths turned towards the woods, seem to be lying in wait. The machine guns, from their hiding places, stare fixedly at the horizon. All is ready for an attack. Why is none made? What are they waiting for?

They await orders from headquarters, but none come.

And yet it is only a short distance to headquarters, to that beautiful Louis XIII chateau whose red brick walls, washed by the rain, are seen half way up the hill, glistening through the thickets. Truly a princely dwelling, well worthy of bearing the banner of a Marshal of France. Upon an artificial pond which sparkles like a mirror, swans are swimming, and under the pagoda-shaped roof of a large aviary, peacocks and golden pheasants strut about, spreading their wings and sending their shrill cries through the foliage. Though the owners of the house have departed, nowhere is there a perceptible sign of that ruin and desolation which war brings in its train; not the smallest flower dotting the lawn has been destroyed and it is indescribably charming to observe. Such evenly trimmed shrubbery, such silent avenues of shade; yet so near the battlefield! The scene is peaceful. Were it not for the flag floating from the top of the roof, and the sight of two sentinels before the gate, one would never believe headquarters were here.

In the dining room, whose windows front the entrance of the chateau, is seen a partly cleared table—bottles uncorked, tarnished empty glasses resting upon the wrinkled cloth—in short, every indication that a repast is ended. The guests have departed; but in a side room loud voices are heard, peals of laughter, the rolling of billiard balls, and the clinking of glasses. The Marshal has just started upon his game, and that is why the army is waiting for orders. Once the Marshal has begun, the heavens might fall, but nothing on earth will hinder him from finishing his game.

For if the mighty soldier has a single weakness, it is his fondness for billiards. There he stands, as grave as though a battle had begun, in full uniform, his breast covered with decorations; his repast, the grog he has drunk, and the excitement of the game animate him. His eyes sparkle, and his cheek-bones are flushed. About him gather his aides-de-camp, most assiduous in their attentions, deferential and overcome with admiration at each of his shots. When the Marshal makes a point, they lunge towards the mark. When the Marshal desires a drink, each one rushes to prepare his grog. Such a rustling of epaulettes and panaches; such a rattling of crosses and aiguillettes.

How these flunkies bow and smile. What elegance and charm of manner. And such embroideries; so many new uniforms in this lofty chamber carved in oak, opening upon parks and courts of honor. It reminds one of these autumns of Compiègne, and makes him forget, for a moment, those figures in muddied cloaks, gathered yonder in the roads, making such somber groups as they wait in the rain.

The Marshal's adversary is a staff officer, a little captain with curls, laces and light gloves; he is an excellent shot at billiards, and could beat all the marshals on earth, but he understands his chief, and exercises all his skill in playing so that he shall neither win nor seem to lose, too readily. Evidently an officer with a future.

Beware, Captain. The Marshal is five points ahead. If you can complete the game as you have begun it, your promotion is surer than it would be, were you standing outside with the others, beneath those torrents of water. It would be a pity, too, to soil that fine uniform.

The game is fascinating. The balls roll, graze, pass; they rebound. Every moment the play grows more interesting. A flash of light is seen in the sky, and the report of a cannon is heard. A heavy rumbling sound shakes the windows. Everyone starts and casts an uneasy glance about. The Marshal alone remains unmoved. He sees nothing, hears nothing, for, leaning over the table, he is about to make a magnificent draw shot. Draw shots are his forte!

Again that flash! Again! From the cannon, fresh reports, and closer together. The aides-de-camp run to the window. Are the Prussians attacking?

"Let them!" says the Marshal, chalking his cue. "Your turn, Captain."

The staff glows with admiration. Turenne, asleep on the gun-carriage, was nothing compared to this marshal, calmly absorbed in his game at the moment of action. But the tumult increases. The rattling of the machine guns mingles with the blast of the cannon and the rumbling of steady volleys. A reddish cloud, dark at the edges, rises from the further end of the lawn. All the rear of the park is ablaze. Frightened peacocks and pheasants shriek in the aviary. Arabian horses, in their stalls, scent the powder and rear in terror. At headquarters a general commotion begins. Despatch follows despatch. Messengers arrive at a gallop. Everywhere they are asking for the Marshal.

But the Marshal remains unapproachable. Nothing —nothing in the world could hinder him from finishing a game once begun.

"Your play, Captain . . ."

But the captain is distracted. He loses his head; forgets where he is, and he makes two successive runs which almost win the game for him. The Marshal is furious. Surprise and indignation mark his features. At this very moment a horse gallops into the courtyard at full speed. An aide-de-camp, covered with mud, forces the sentry, makes one bound over the stone steps crying, "Marshal, Marshal!" The Marshal, red and swelling with anger, appears at the window, cue in hand.

"Who is there? What is it? Is there no sentry there?"

"But, Marshal . . ."

"Oh, yes, yes—later—let them wait for my orders— in God's name!"

And the window closes with a bang.

Let them wait for his orders. That is exactly what they are doing, those poor fellows. The wind drives rain and grapeshot in their faces. Battalions are slaughtered, while others stand useless, bearing arms, unable to understand why they remain inactive. They wait for orders. But men may die without orders, and these men die in hundreds, falling behind bushes, dropping in trenches in front of that great silent chateau. Even after their death, the grapeshot continues to lacerate their bodies; from those gaping wounds flows a silent stream—the generous blood of France. Above, in the billiard room, all is excited as upon the battlefield. The Marshal has regained his advantage, and the little captain is playing like a lion.

Seventeen! eighteen! nineteen! Scarcely time to mark the points. The sound of battle grows nearer and nearer. The Marshal has but one more point to play. Already shells are falling in the park. One has burst in the pond. The glassy sheen reddens, and a terrified swan is seen swimming amid a whirl of bloody plumage. And now the last shot.

And then—deep silence. Only the sound of rain falling; only an indistinct rumbling noise at the foot of the hill, and along the muddy roads a sound like the tramping of hurrying herds. The army is utterly routed. The Marshal has won his game.

The Test

BY ANGELICA GIBBS

On the afternoon Marian took her second driver's test, Mrs. Ericson went with her. "It's probably better to have someone a little older with you," Mrs. Ericson said as Marian slipped into the driver's seat beside her. "Perhaps the last time your Cousin Bill made you nervous, talking too much on the way."

"Yes, Ma'am," Marian said in her soft unaccented voice. "They probably do like it better if a white person shows up with you."

"Oh, I don't think it's *that*," Mrs. Ericson began, and subsided after a glance at the girl's set profile. Marian drove the car slowly through the shady suburban streets. It was one of the first hot days in June, and when they reached the boulevard they found it crowded with cars headed for the beaches.

"Do you want me to drive?" Mrs. Ericson asked. "I'll be glad to if you're feeling jumpy." Marian shook her head. Mrs. Ericson watched her dark, competent hands and wondered for the thousandth time how the house had ever managed to get along without her, or how she had lived through those earlier years when her household had been presided over by a series of slatternly white girls who had considered housework demeaning and the care of children an added insult. "You drive beautifully, Marian," she said. "Now, don't think of the last time. Anybody would slide on a steep hill on a wet day like that."

"It takes four mistakes to flunk you," Marian said. "I don't remember doing all the things the inspector marked down on my blank."

"People say that they only want you to slip them a little something," Mrs. Ericson said doubtfully.

"No," Marian said. "That would only make it worse, Mrs. Ericson, I know."

The car turned right, at a traffic signal, into a side road and slid up to the curb at the rear of a short line of parked cars. The inspectors had not arrived yet.

"You have the papers?" Mrs. Ericson asked. Marian took them out of her bag: her learner's permit, the car registration, and her birth certificate. They settled down to the dreary business of waiting.

"It will be marvelous to have someone dependable to drive the children to school every day," Mrs. Ericson said.

Marian looked up from the list of driving requirements she had been studying. "It'll make things simpler at the house, won't it?" she said.

"Oh, Marian," Mrs. Ericson exclaimed, "if I could only pay you half of what you're worth!"

"Now, Mrs. Ericson," Marian said firmly. They looked at each other and smiled with affection.

Two cars with official insignia on their doors stopped across the street. The inspectors leaped out, very brisk and military in their neat uniforms. Marian's hands tightened on the wheel. "There's the one who flunked me last time," she whispered, pointing to a stocky, self-important man who had begun to shout directions at the driver at the head of the line. "Oh, Mrs. Ericson."

"Now, Marian," Mrs. Ericson said. They smiled at each other again, rather weakly.

The inspector who finally reached their car was not the stocky one but a genial, middle-aged man who grinned broadly as he thumbed over their papers. Mrs. Ericson started to get out of the car. "Don't you want to come along?" the inspector asked. "Mandy and I don't mind company."

Mrs. Ericson was bewildered for a moment. "No," she said, and stepped to the curb. "I might make Marian self-conscious. She's a fine driver, Inspector."

"Sure thing," the inspector said, winking at Mrs. Ericson. He slid into the seat beside Marian. "Turn right at the corner, Mandy-Lou."

From the curb, Mrs. Ericson watched the car move smoothly up the street.

The inspector made notations in a small black book. "Age?" he inquired presently, as they drove along.

"Twenty-seven."

He looked at Marian out of the corner of his eye. "Old enough to have quite a flock of pickaninnies, eh?"

Marian did not answer.

"Left at this corner," the inspector said, "and park between that truck and the green Buick."

The two cars were very close together, but Marian squeezed in between them without too much maneuvering. "Driven before, Mandy-Lou?" the inspector asked.

"Yes, sir. I had a license for three years in Pennsylvania."

"Why do you want to drive a car?"

"My employer needs me to take her children to and from school."

"Sure you don't really want to sneak out nights to meet some young blood?" the inspector asked. He laughed as Marian shook her head.

"Let's see you take a left at the corner and then turn around in the middle of the next block," the inspector said. He began to whistle "Swanee River." "Make you homesick?" he asked.

Marian put out her hand, swung around neatly in the street, and headed back in the direction from which they had come. "No," she said. "I was born in Scranton, Pennsylvania."

The inspector feigned astonishment. "You-all ain't Southern?" he said. "Well, dog my cats if I didn't think you-all came from down yondah."

"No, sir," Marian said.

"Turn onto Main Street and let's see how you-all does in heavier traffic."

They followed a line of cars along Main Street for several blocks until they came in sight of a concrete bridge which arched high over the railroad tracks.

"Read that sign at the end of the bridge," the inspector said.

" 'Proceed with caution. Dangerous in slippery weather,' " Marian said.

"You-all sho can read fine," the inspector exclaimed. "Where d'you learn to do that, Mandy?"

"I got my college degree last year," Marian said. Her voice was not quite steady.

As the car crept up the slope of the bridge the inspector burst out laughing. He laughed so hard he could scarcely give his next direction. "Stop here," he said, wiping his eyes, "then start 'er up again. Mandy got her degree, did she? Dog my cats!"

Marian pulled up beside the curb. She put the car in neutral, pulled on the emergency, waited a moment, and then put the car into gear again. Her face was set. As she released the brake her foot slipped off the clutch pedal and the engine stalled.

"Now, Mistress Mandy," the inspector said, "remember your degree."

"*Damn* you!" Marian cried. She started the car with a jerk.

The inspector lost his joviality in an instant. "Return to the starting place, please," he said, and made four very black crosses at random in the squares on Marian's application blank.

Mrs. Ericson was waiting at the curb where they had left her. As Marian stopped the car, the inspector jumped out and brushed past her, his face purple. "What happened?" Mrs. Ericson asked, looked after him with alarm.

Marian stared down at the wheel and her lip trembled.

"Oh, Marian, *again?*" Mrs. Ericson said.

Marian nodded. "In a sort of different way," she said, and slid over to the right-hand side of the car.

The Disabled Soldier / Goldsmith

The Disabled Soldier

BY OLIVER GOLDSMITH

📖 📖 📖

No observation is more common, and at the same time more true, than that one half of the world are ignorant how the other half lives. The misfortunes of the great are held up to engage our attention; are enlarged upon in tones of declamation; and the world is called upon to gaze at the noble sufferers: the great, under the pressure of calamity, are conscious of several others sympathising with their distress; and have, at once, the comfort of admiration and pity.

There is nothing magnanimous in bearing misfortunes with fortitude, when the whole world is looking on: men in such circumstances will act bravely even from motives of vanity: but he who, in the vale of obscurity, can brave adversity; who without friends to encourage, acquaintances to pity, or even without hope to alleviate his misfortunes, can behave with tranquillity and indifference, is truly great: whether peasant or courtier, he deserves admiration, and should be held up for our imitation and respect.

While the slightest inconveniences of the great are magnified into calamities; while tragedy mouths out their sufferings in all the strains of eloquence, the miseries of the poor are entirely disregarded; and yet some of the lower ranks of people undergo more real hardships in one day, than those of a more exalted station suffer in their whole lives. It is inconceivable what difficulties the meanest of our common sailors and soldiers endure without murmuring or regret; without passionately declaiming against providence, or calling their fellows to be gazers of their intrepidity. Every day is to them a day of misery, and yet they entertain their hard fate without repining.

With what indignation do I hear an Ovid, a Cicero, or a Rabutin complain of their misfortunes and hardships, whose greatest calamity was that of being unable to visit a certain spot of earth, to which they had foolishly attached an idea of happiness. Their distresses were pleasures, compared to what many of the adventuring poor every day endure without murmuring. They ate, drank, and slept; they had slaves to attend them, and were sure of subsistence for life; while many of their fellow creatures are obliged to wander without a friend to comfort or assist them, and even without shelter from the severity of the season.

I have been led into these reflections from accidentally meeting, some days ago, a poor fellow, whom I knew when a boy, dressed in a sailor's jacket, and begging at one of the outlets of the town, with a wooden leg. I knew him to have been honest and industrious when in the country, and was curious to learn what had reduced him to his present situation. Wherefore, after giving him what I thought proper, I desired to know the history of his life and misfortunes, and the manner in which he was reduced to his present distress. The disabled soldier, for such he was, though dressed in a sailor's habit, scratching his head, and leaning on his crutch, put himself into an attitude to comply with my request, and gave me his history as follows:

"As for my misfortunes, master, I can't pretend to have gone through any more than other folks; for, except for the loss of my limb, and my being obliged to beg, I don't know any reason, thank Heaven, that I have to complain. There is Bill Tibbs, of our regiment, he has lost both his legs, and an eye to boot; but, thank Heaven, it is not so bad with me yet.

"I was born in Shropshire; my father was a la-
bourer, and died when I was five years old, so I was
put upon the parish. As he had been a wandering sort
of man, the parishioners were not able to tell to what
parish I belonged, or where I was born, so they sent
me to another parish, and that parish sent me to a
third. I thought in my heart, they kept sending me
about so long, that they would not let me be born in
any parish at all; but at last, however, they fixed me.
I had some disposition to be a scholar, and was resolved at least to know my letters: but the master of
the workhouse put me to business as soon as I was
able to handle a mallet; and here I lived an easy kind
of life for five years. I only wrought ten hours in the
day and had my meat and drink provided for my
labour. It was true, I was not suffered to stir out of
the house, for fear, as they said, I should run away;
but what of that? I had the liberty of the whole house,
and the yard before the door, and that was enough for
me. I was then bound out to a farmer, where I was
up both early and late; but I ate and drank well; and
liked my business well enough, till he died, when I was
obliged to provide for myself; so I was resolved to go
seek my fortune.

"In this manner I went from town to town, worked
when I could get employment, and starved when I
could get none; when, happening one day to go through
a field belonging to a justice of the peace, I spied a
hare crossing the path just before me; and I believe
the devil put it into my head to fling my stick at it.
Well, what will you have on't? I killed the hare, and
was bringing it away, when the justice himself met me;
he called me a poacher and a villain, and collaring me,
desired I would give an account of myself. I fell upon
my knees, begged his worship's pardon, and began to
give a full account of all that I knew of my breed,
seed, and generation; but though I gave a very true
account, the justice said I could give no account; so
I was indicted at the sessions, found guilty of being

poor, and sent up to London to Newgate, in order to
be transported as a vagabond.

"People may say this and that of being in jail, but
for my part, I found Newgate as agreeable a place as
ever I was in all my life. I had my belly full to eat
and drink, and did no work at all. This kind of life
was too good to last forever; so I was taken out of
prison, after five months, put on board of ship, and
sent off, with two hundred more, to the plantations.
We had but an indifferent passage, for being all con-
fined to the hold, more than a hundred of our people
died for want of sweet air; and those that remained
were sickly enough, God knows. When we came
ashore we were sold to the planters, and I was bound
for seven years more. As I was no scholar, for I did
not know my letters, I was obliged to work among
the Negroes; and I served out my time, as in duty
bound to do.

"When my time was expired, I worked my passage
home, and glad I was to see old England again, because I loved my country. I was afraid, however, that
I should be indicted for a vagabond once more, so
did not much care to go down into the country, but
kept about the town, and did little jobs when I could
get them.

"I was very happy in this manner for some time
till one evening, coming home from work, two men
knocked me down, and then desired me to stand. They
belonged to a press-gang. I was carried before the
justice, and as I could give no account of myself, I
had no choice left, whether to go on board a man-of-
war, or list for a solider. I chose the latter, and in this
post of a gentleman, I served two campaigns in
Flanders, was at the battles of Val and Fontenoy,
and received but one wound through the breast here;
but the doctor of our regiment soon made me well
again.

"When the peace came on I was discharged; and as
I could not work, because my wound was sometimes

troublesome, I listed for a landman in the East India Company's service. I have fought the French in six pitched battles; and I verily believe that if I could read or write, our captain would have made me a corporal. But it was not my good fortune to have any promotion, for I soon fell sick, and so got leave to return home again with forty pounds in my pocket. This was at the beginning of the present war, and I hoped to be set on shore, and to have the pleasure of spending my money; but the Government wanted men, and so I was pressed for a sailor, before ever I could set foot on shore.

"The boatswain found me, as he said, an obstinate fellow: he swore he knew that I understood my business well, but that I shammed Abraham to be idle; but God knows, I knew nothing of sea-business, and he beat me without considering what he was about. I had still, however, my forty pounds, and that was some comfort to me under every beating; and the money I might have had to this day, but that our ship was taken by the French, and so I lost all.

"Our crew was carried into Brest, and many of them died, because they were not used to life in a jail; but, for my part, it was nothing to me, for I was seasoned. One night, as I was asleep on the bed of boards, with a warm blanket about me, for I always loved to lie well, I was awakened by the boatswain, who had a dark lantern in his hand. 'Jack,' says he to me, 'will you knock out the French sentry's brains?' 'I don't care,' says I, striving to keep myself awake, 'if I lend a hand.' 'Then follow me,' says he, 'and I hope we shall do business.' So up I got, and tied my blanket, which was all the clothes I had, about my middle, and went with him to fight the Frenchman. I hate the French, because they are all slaves, and wear wooden shoes.

"Though we had no arms, one Englishman is able to beat five French at any time; so we went down to the door where both sentries were posted, and rushing upon them, seized their arms in a moment, and knocked them down. From thence nine of us ran together to the quay, and seizing the first boat we met, got out of the harbour and put to sea. We had not been here three days before we were taken up by the *Dorset* privateer, who were glad of so many good hands; and we consented to run our chance. However, we had not as much luck as we expected. In three days we fell in with the *Pompadour* privateer of forty guns, while we had but twenty-three, so to it we went, yard-arm and yard-arm. The fight lasted three hours, and I verily believe we should have taken the Frenchman, had we but some more men left behind; but unfortunately we lost all our men just as we were going to get the victory.

"I was once more in the power of the French, and I believe it would have gone hard with me had I been brought back to Brest; but by good fortune we were retaken by the *Viper*. I had almost forgotten to tell you, that in that engagement, I was wounded in two places: I lost four fingers off the left hand, and my leg was shot off. If I had had the good fortune to have lost my leg and the use of my hand on board a king's ship, and not aboard a privateer, I should have been entitled to clothing and maintenance during the rest of my life; but that was not my chance: one man is born with a silver spoon in his mouth, and another with a wooden ladle. However, Blessed be God, I enjoy good health, and will for ever love liberty and old England. Liberty, property, and Old England, for ever, huzza!"

Thus saying, he limped off, leaving me in admiration at his intrepidity and content; nor could I avoid acknowledging that an habitual acquaintance with misery serves better than philosophy to teach us to despise it.

Virtuoso

BY HERBERT GOLDSTONE

◫ ◫ ◫

"Sir?"

The Maestro continued to play, not looking up from the keys.

"Sir, I was wondering if you would explain this apparatus to me."

The Maestro stopped playing, his thin body stiffly relaxed on the bench. His long supple fingers floated off the keyboard.

"Apparatus?" He turned and smiled at the robot. "Do you mean the piano, Rollo?"

"This machine that produces varying sounds. I would like some information about it, its operation and purpose. It is not included in my reference data."

The Maestro lit a cigarette. He preferred to do it himself. One of his first orders to Rollo when the robot was delivered two days before had been to disregard his built-in instructions on the subject.

"I'd hardly call a piano a machine, Rollo," he smiled, "although technically you are correct. It is actually, I suppose, a machine designed to produce sounds of graduated pitch and tone, singly or in groups."

"I assimilated that much by observation," Rollo replied in a brassy baritone which no longer sent tiny tremors up the Maestro's spine. "Wires of different thickness and tautness struck by felt-covered hammers activated by manually operated levers arranged in a horizontal panel."

"A very cold-blooded description of one of man's

nobler works," the Maestro remarked dryly. "You make Mozart and Chopin mere laboratory technicians."

"Mozart? Chopin?" The duralloy sphere that was Rollo's head shone stark and featureless, its immediate surface unbroken but for twin vision lenses. "The terms are not included in my memory banks."

"No, not yours, Rollo," the Maestro said softly. "Mozart and Chopin are not for vacuum tubes and fuses and copper wire. They are for flesh and blood and human tears."

"I do not understand," Rollo droned.

"Well," the Maestro said, smoke curling lazily from his nostrils, "they are two of the humans who compose, or design successions of notes—varying sounds, that is, produced by the piano or by other instruments, machines that produce other types of sounds of fixed pitch and tone.

"Sometimes these instruments, as we call them, are played, or operated, individually: sometimes in groups —orchestras, as we refer to them—and the sounds blend together, they harmonize. That is, they have an orderly, mathematical relationship to each other which results in . . ."

The Maestro threw up his hands.

"I never imagined," he chuckled, "that I would some day struggle so mightily, and so futilely, to explain music to a robot!"

"Music?"

"Yes, Rollo. The sounds produced by this machine and others of the same category are called music."

"What is the purpose of music, sir?"

"Purpose?"

The Maestro crushed the cigarette in an ash tray. He turned to the keyboard of the concert grand and flexed his fingers briefly.

"Listen, Rollo."

The wraithlike fingers glided and wove the opening bars of "Clair de Lune," slender and delicate as spider silk. Rollo stood rigid, the fluorescent light over the music rack casting a bluish jeweled sheen over his towering bulk, shimmering in the amber vision lenses.

The Maestro drew his hands back from the keys and the subtle thread of melody melted reluctantly into silence.

"Claude Debussy," the Maestro said. "One of our mechanics of an era long past. He designed that succession of tones many years ago. What do you think of it?"

Rollo did not answer at once.

"The sounds were well formed," he replied finally. "They did not jar my auditory senses as some do."

The Maestro laughed. "Rollo, you may not realize it, but you're a wonderful critic."

"This music then," Rollo droned. "Its purpose is to give pleasure to humans?"

"Exactly," the Maestro said. "Sounds well formed, that do not jar the auditory senses as some do. Marvelous! It should be carved in marble over the entrance of New Carnegie Hall."

"I do not understand. Why should my definition—?"

The Maestro waved a hand. "No matter, Rollo. No matter."

"Sir?"

"Yes, Rollo?"

"Those sheets of paper you sometimes place before you on the piano. They are the plans of the composer indicating which sounds are to be produced by the piano and in what order?"

"Just so. We call each sound a note; combinations of notes we call chords."

"Each dot, then, indicates a sound to be made?"

"Perfectly correct, my man of metal."

Rollo stared straight ahead. The Maestro felt a peculiar sense of wheels turning within that impregnable sphere.

"Sir, I have scanned my memory banks and find no specific or implied instructions against it. I should like to be taught how to produce these notes on the piano. I request that you feed the correlation between those dots and the levers of the panel into my memory banks."

The Maestro peered at him, amazed. A slow grin traveled across his face.

"Done!" he exclaimed. "It's been many years since pupils helped gray these ancient locks, but I have the feeling that you, Rollo, will prove a most fascinating student. To instill the Muse into metal and machinery . . . I accept the challenge gladly!"

He rose, touched the cool latent power of Rollo's arm.

"Sit down here, my Rolleindex Personal Robot, Model M-e. We shall start Beethoven spinning in his grave—or make musical history."

More than an hour later the Maestro yawned and looked at his watch.

"It's late," he spoke into the end of the yawn. "These old eyes are not tireless like yours, my friend." He touched Rollo's shoulder. "You have the complete fundamentals of musical notation in your memory banks, Rollo. That's a good night's lesson, particularly when I recall how long it took me to acquire the same amount of information. Tomorrow we'll attempt to put those awesome fingers of yours to work."

He stretched. "I'm going to bed," he said. "Will you lock up and put out the lights?"

Rollo rose from the bench. "Yes, sir," he droned. "I have a request."

"What can I do for my star pupil?"

"May I attempt to create some sounds with the keyboard tonight? I will do so very softly so as not to disturb you."

"Tonight? Aren't you—?" Then the Maestro smiled. "You must pardon me, Rollo. It's still a bit difficult for me to realize that sleep has no meaning for you."

He hesitated, rubbing his chin. "Well, I suppose a good teacher should not discourage impatience to learn. All right, Rollo, but please be careful." He patted the polished mahogany. "This piano and I have been together for many years. I'd hate to see its teeth knocked out by those sledge-hammer digits of yours. Lightly, my friend, very lightly."

"Yes, sir."

The Maestro fell asleep with a faint smile on his lips, dimly aware of the shy, tentative notes that Rollo was coaxing forth.

Then gray fog closed in and he was in that half-world where reality is dreamlike and dreams are real. It was soft and feathery and lavender clouds and sounds were rolling and washing across his mind in flowing waves.

Where? The mist drew back a bit and he was in red velvet and deep and the music swelled and broke over him.

He smiled.

My recording. Thank you, thank you, thank—

The Maestro snapped erect, threw the covers aside.

He sat on the edge of the bed, listening.

He groped for his robe in the darkness, shoved bony feet into his slippers.

He crept, trembling uncontrollably, to the door of his studio and stood there, thin and brittle in the robe.

The light over the music rack was an eerie island in the brown shadows of the studio. Rollo sat at the keyboard, prim, inhuman, rigid, twin lenses focused somewhere off into the shadows.

The massive feet working the pedals, arms and hands flashing and glinting—they were living entities, separate, somehow, from the machined perfection of his body.

The music rack was empty.

A copy of Beethoven's "Appassionata" lay closed on the bench. It had been, the Maestro remembered, in a pile of sheet music on the piano.

Rollo was playing it.

He was creating it, breathing it, drawing it through silver flame.

Time became meaningless, suspended in midair.

The Maestro didn't realize he was weeping until Rollo finished the sonata.

The robot turned to look at the Maestro. "The sounds," he droned. "They pleased you?"

The Maestro's lips quivered. "Yes, Rollo," he replied at last. "They pleased me." He fought the lump in his throat.

He picked up the music in fingers that shook.

"This," he murmured. "Already?"

"It has been added to my store of data," Rollo replied. "I applied the principles you explained to me to these plans. It was not very difficult."

The Maestro swallowed as he tried to speak. "It was not very difficult . . ." he repeated softly.

The old man sank down slowly onto the bench next to Rollo, stared silently at the robot as though seeing him for the first time.

Rollo got to his feet.

The Maestro let his fingers rest on the keys, strangely foreign now.

"Music!" he breathed. "I may have heard it that way in my soul. I know Beethoven did!"

He looked up at the robot, a growing excitement in his face.

"Rollo," he said, his voice straining to remain calm. "You and I have some work to do tomorrow on your memory banks."

Sleep did not come again that night.

He strode briskly into the studio the next morning. Rollo was vacuuming the carpet. The Maestro preferred carpets to the new dust-free plastics, which felt somehow profane to his feet.

The Maestro's house was, in fact, an oasis of anachronisms in a desert of contemporary antiseptic efficiency.

"Well, are you ready for work, Rollo?" he asked. "We have a lot to do, you and I. I have such plans for you, Rollo—great plans!"

Rollo, for once, did not reply.

"I have asked them all to come here this afternoon," the Maestro went on. "Conductors, concert pianists, composers, my manager. All the giants of music, Rollo. Wait until they hear you play."

Rollo switched off the vacuum and stood quietly.

"You'll play for them right here this afternoon." The Maestro's voice was high-pitched, breathless. "The 'Appassionata' again, I think. Yes, that's it. I must see their faces!

"Then we'll arrange a recital to introduce you to the public and the critics and then a major concerto with one of the big orchestras. We'll have it telecast around the world, Rollo. It can be arranged.

"Think of it, Rollo, just think of it! The greatest piano virtuoso of all time . . . a robot! It's completely fantastic and completely wonderful. I feel like an explorer at the edge of a new world."

He walked feverishly back and forth.

"Then recordings, of course. My entire repertoire, Rollo, and more. So much more!"

"Sir?"

The Maestro's face shone as he looked up at him. "Yes, Rollo?"

"In my built-in instructions, I have the option of rejecting any action which I consider harmful to my owner," the robot's words were precise, carefully selected. "Last night you wept. That is one of the indications I am instructed to consider in making my decisions."

The Maestro gripped Rollo's thick, superbly molded arm.

"Rollo, you don't understand. That was for the moment. It was petty of me, childish!"

"I beg your pardon, sir, but I must refuse to approach the piano again."

The Maestro stared at him, unbelieving, pleading.

"Rollo, you can't! The world must hear you!"

"No, sir." The amber lenses almost seemed to soften.

"The piano is not a machine," that powerful inhuman voice droned. "To me, yes. I can translate the notes into sounds at a glance. From only a few I am able to grasp at once the composer's conception. It is easy for me."

Rollo towered magnificently over the Maestro's bent form.

"I can also grasp," the brassy monotone rolled through the studio, "that this . . . music is not for robots. It is for man. To me it is easy, yes. . . . It was not meant to be easy."

The Hollow of the Three Hills

BY NATHANIEL HAWTHORNE

In those strange old times, when fantastic dreams and madmen's reveries were realised among the actual circumstances of life, two persons met together at an appointed hour and place. One was a lady, graceful in form and fair of feature, though pale and troubled, and smitten with an untimely blight in what should have been the fullest bloom of her years; the other was an ancient and meanly-dressed woman, of ill-favoured aspect, and so withered, shrunken and decrepit, that even the space since she began to decay must have exceeded the ordinary term of human existence. In the spot where they encountered, no mortal could observe them. Three little hills stood by each other, and down in the midst of them sunk a hollow basin, almost mathematically circular, two or three hundred feet in breadth, and of such depth that a stately cedar might but just be visible above the sides. Dwarf pines were numerous upon the hills, and partly fringed the outer verge of the intermediate hollow; within which there was nothing but the brown grass of October, and here and there a tree-trunk, that had fallen long ago, and lay mouldering with no green successor from its roots. One of these masses of decaying wood, formerly a majestic oak, rested close beside a pool of green and sluggish water at the bottom of the basin. Such scenes as this (so grey tradition tells) were once the resort of a power of evil and his plighted subjects; and here, at midnight or

on the dim verge of evening, they were said to stand
round the mantling pool, disturbing its putrid waters
in the performance of an impious baptismal rite. The
chill beauty of an autumnal sunset was now gilding
the three hill-tops, whence a paler tint stole down
their sides into the hollow.

"Here is our pleasant meeting come to pass," said
the aged crone, "according as thou hast desired. Say
quickly what thou wouldest have of me, for there is
but a short hour that we may tarry here."

As the old, withered woman spoke, a smile glimmered on her countenance, like lamplight on the wall
of a sepulchre. The lady trembled, and cast her eyes
upward to the verge of the basin, as if meditating to
return with her purpose unaccomplished. But it was
not so ordained.

"I am a stranger in this land, as you know," said
she, at length. "Whence I come it matters not; but I
have left those behind me with whom my fate was
intimately bound, and from whom I am cut off for
ever. There is a weight in my bosom that I cannot
away with, and I have come hither to inquire of their
welfare."

"And who is there by this green pool that can bring
thee news from the ends of the earth?" cried the old
woman, peering into the lady's face. "Not from my
lips mayest thou hear these tidings; yet, be thou bold,
and the daylight shall not pass away from yonder hill-
top before thy wish be granted."

"I will do your bidding though I die," replied the
lady, desperately.

The old woman seated herself on the trunk of the
fallen tree, threw aside the hood that shrouded her
grey locks, and beckoned her companion to draw near.

"Kneel down," she said, "and lay your forehead on
my knees."

She hesitated a moment, but the anxiety that had
long been kindling burned fiercely up within her. As
she knelt down, the border of her garment was dipped

into the pool; she laid her forehead on the old woman's knees, and the latter drew a cloak about the lady's face, so that she was in darkness. Then she heard the muttered words of prayer, in the midst of which she started, and would have arisen.

"Let me flee—let me flee and hide myself, that they may not look upon me!" she cried. But, with returning recollection, she hushed herself, and was still as death.

For it seemed as if other voices—familiar in infancy, and unforgotten through many wanderings, and in all the vicissitudes of her heart and fortune—were mingling with the accents of the prayer. At first the words were faint and indistinct, not rendered so by distance, but rather resembling the dim pages of a book which we strive to read by an imperfect and gradually brightening light. In such a manner, as the prayer proceeded, did those voices strengthen upon the ear; till at length the petition ended, and the conversation of an aged man, and of a woman broken and decayed like himself, became distinctly audible to the lady as she knelt. But those strangers appeared not to stand in the hollow depth between the three hills. Their voices were encompassed and re-echoed by the walls of a chamber, the windows of which were rattling in the breeze; the regular vibration of a clock, the crackling of a fire, and the tinkling of the embers as they fell among the ashes, rendered the scene almost as vivid as if painted to the eye. By a melancholy hearth sat these two old people, the man calmly despondent, the woman querulous and tearful, and their words were all of sorrow. They spoke of a daughter, a wanderer they knew not where, bearing dishonour along with her, and leaving shame and affliction to bring their grey heads to the grave. They alluded also to other and more recent woe, but in the midst of their talk their voices seemed to melt into the sound of the wind sweeping mournful among the autumn leaves; and when the lady lifted her eyes, there was she kneeling in the hollow between three hills.

"A weary and lonesome time yonder old couple have of it," remarked the old woman, smiling in the lady's face.

"And did you also hear them?" exclaimed she, a sense of intolerable humiliation triumphing over her agony and fear.

"Yea; and we have yet more to hear," replied the old woman. "Wherefore cover thy face quickly."

Again the withered hag poured forth the monotonous words of a prayer that was not meant to be acceptable in heaven; and soon in the pauses of her breath strange murmurings began to thicken, gradually increasing, so as to drown and overpower the charm by which they grew. Shrieks pierced through the obscurity of sound, and were succeeded by the singing of sweet female voices, which in their turn gave way to a wild roar of laughter, broken suddenly by groanings and sobs, forming altogether a ghastly confusion of terror and mourning and mirth. Chains were rattling, fierce and stern voices uttered threats, and the scourge resounded at their command. All these noises deepened and became substantial to the listener's ear, till she could distinguish every soft and dreamy accent of the love songs, that died causelessly into funeral hymns. She shuddered at the unprovoked wrath which blazed up like the spontaneous kindling of flame, and she grew faint at the fearful merriment raging miserably around her. In the midst of this wild scene, where unbound passions jostled each other in a drunken career, there was one solemn voice of a man, and a manly and melodious voice it might once have been. He went to and fro continually, and his feet sounded upon the floor. In each member of that frenzied company, whose own burning thoughts had become their exclusive world, he sought an auditor for the story of his individual wrong, and interrupted their laughter and tears as his reward of scorn or pity. He spoke of women's perfidy, of a wife who had broken her holiest vows, of a home and heart made desolate. Even as he went on, the shout, the laugh, and shriek, the sob, rose up in unison, till they changed into the hollow, fitful, and uneven sound of the wind, as it fought among the pine-trees on those three lonely hills. The lady looked up, and there was the withered woman smiling in her face.

"Couldest thou have thought there were such merry times in a madhouse?" inquired the latter.

"True, true," said the lady to herself, "there is mirth within its walls, but misery, misery without."

"Wouldest thou hear more?" demanded the old woman.

"There is one other voice I would fain listen to again," replied the lady faintly.

"Then lay down thy head speedily upon my knees, that thou mayest get thee hence before the hour be past."

The golden skirts of day were yet lingering upon the hills, but deep shades obscured the hollow and the pool, as if sombre night were rising thence to overspread the world. Again that evil woman began to weave her spell. Long did it proceed unanswered, till the knolling of a bell stole in among the intervals of her words, like a clang that had travelled far over valley and rising ground, and was just ready to die in the air. The lady shook upon her companion's knees as she heard that boding sound. Stronger it grew and sadder, and deepened into the tone of a death-bell knolling dolefully from some ivy-mantled tower, and bearing tidings of mortality and woe to the cottage, to the hall and to the solitary wayfarer, that all might weep for the doom appointed in turn to them. Then came a measured tread, passing slowly, slowly on, as of mourners with a coffin, their garments trailing on the ground, so that the ear could measure the length of their melancholy array. Before them went the priest reading the burial service, while the leaves of his book were rustling in the breeze. And though no voice but his was heard to speak aloud, still there were revilings and anathemas whispered, but distinct, from women and from men, breathed against the daughter who had wrung the aged hearts of her parents, the wife who had betrayed the trusting fondness of her husband, the mother who had sinned against natural affection and left her child to die. The sweeping sound of the funeral train faded away like a thin vapour, and the wind, that just before had seemed to shake the coffin-pall, moaned sadly round the verge of the hollow between three hills. But when the old woman stirred the kneeling lady she lifted not her head.

"Here has been a sweet hour's sport," said the withered crone, chuckling to herself.

The Boy Who Drew Cats

BY LAFCADIO HEARN

A long, long time ago, in a small country village in Japan, there lived a poor farmer and his wife, who were very good people. They had a number of children, and found it very hard to feed them all. The elder son was strong enough when only fourteen years old to help his father; and the little girls learned to help their mother almost as soon as they could walk.

But the youngest, a little boy, did not seem to be fit for hard work. He was very clever—cleverer than all his brothers and sisters; but he was quite weak and small, and people said he could never grow very big. So his parents thought it would be better for him to become a priest than to become a farmer. They took him with them to the village-temple one day, and asked the good old priest who lived there if he would have their little boy for his acolyte, and teach him all that a priest ought to know.

The old man spoke kindly to the lad, and asked him some hard questions. So clever were the answers that the priest agreed to take the little fellow into the temple as an acolyte, and to educate him for the priesthood.

The boy learned quickly what the old priest taught him, and was very obedient in most things. But he had one fault. He liked to draw cats during study-hours, and to draw cats even where cats ought not to have been drawn at all.

Whenever he found himself alone, he drew cats. He drew them on the margins of the priest's books, and on all the screens of the temple, and on the walls, and on the pillars. Several times the priest told him this was not right; but he did not stop drawing cats. He drew them because he could not really help it. He had what is called "the genius of an artist," and just for that reason he was not quite fit to be an acolyte;—a good acolyte should study books.

One day after he had drawn some very clever pictures of cats upon a paper screen, the old priest said to him severely: "My boy, you must go away from this temple at once. You will never make a good priest, but perhaps you will become a great artist. Now let me give you a last piece of advice, and be sure you never forget it. *Avoid large places at night;—keep to small!*"

The boy did not know what the priest meant by saying, *"Avoid large places;—keep to small."* He thought and thought, while he was tying up his little bundle of clothes to go away; but he could not understand those words, and he was afraid to speak to the priest any more, except to say goodby.

He left the temple very sorrowfully, and began to wonder what he should do. If he went straight home he felt sure his father would punish him for having been disobedient to the priest; so he was afraid to go home. All at once he remembered that at the next village, twelve miles away, there was a very big temple. He had heard there were several priests at that temple; and he made up his mind to go to them and ask them to take him for their acolyte.

Now that big temple was closed up but the boy did not know this fact. The reason it had been closed up was that a goblin had frightened the priests away, and had taken possession of the place. Some brave warriors had afterward gone to the temple at night to kill the goblin; but they had never been seen alive again. Nobody had ever told these things to the boy;— so he walked all the way to the village hoping to be kindly treated by the priests.

When he got to the village, it was already dark, and all the people were in bed; but he saw the big temple on a hill at the other end of the principal street, and he saw there was a light in the temple. People who tell the story say the goblin used to make that light, in order to tempt lonely travelers to ask for shelter. The boy went at once to the temple, and knocked. There was no sound inside. He knocked and knocked again; but still nobody came. At last he pushed gently at the door, and was quite glad to find that it had not been fastened. So he went in, and saw a lamp burning—but no priest.

He thought some priest would be sure to come very soon, and he sat down and waited. Then he noticed that everything in the temple was gray with dust, and thickly spun over with cobwebs. So he thought to himself that the priests would certainly like to have an acolyte, to keep the place clean. He wondered why they had allowed everything to get so dusty. What most pleased him, however, were some big white screens, good to paint cats upon. Though he was tired, he looked at once for a writing pad, and found one and ground some ink, and began to paint cats.

He painted a great many cats upon the screens; and then he began to feel very, very sleepy. He was just on the point of lying down to sleep beside one of the screens, when he suddenly remembered the words, *"Avoid large places;—keep to small!"*

The temple was very large; he was all alone; and as he thought of these words—though he could not quite understand them—he began to feel for the first time a little afraid; and he resolved to look for a *small place* in which to sleep. He found a little cabinet, with a sliding door, and went into it, and shut himself up. Then he lay down and fell fast asleep.

Very late in the night he was awakened by a most

terrible noise—a noise of fighting and screaming. It was so dreadful that he was afraid even to look through a chink in the little cabinet; he lay very still, holding his breath for fright.

The light that had been in the temple went out; but the awful sounds continued, and became more awful, and all the temple shook. After a long time silence came; but the boy was still afraid to move. He did not move until the light of the morning sun shone into the cabinet through the chinks of the little door.

Then he got out of his hiding place very cautiously, and looked about. The first thing he saw was that all the floor of the temple was covered with blood. And then he saw, lying dead in the middle of it, an enormous, monstrous rat—a goblin-rat—bigger than a cow!

But who or what could have killed it? There was no man or other creature to be seen. Suddenly the boy observed that the mouths of all the cats he had drawn the night before, were red and wet with blood. Then he knew that the goblin had been killed by the cats which he had drawn. And then also, for the first time, he understood why the wise old priest had said to him, *"Avoid large places at night;—keep to small."*

Afterward that boy became a very famous artist. Some of the cats which he drew are still shown to travelers in Japan.

The Exact Science of Matrimony

BY O. HENRY

"As I have told you before," said Jeff Peters, "I never had much confidence in the perfidiousness of woman. As partners or coeducators in the most innocent line of graft they are not trustworthy."

"They deserve the compliment," said I. "I think they are entitled to be called the honest sex."

"Why shouldn't they be?" said Jeff. "They've got the other sex either grafting or working overtime for 'em. They're all right in business until they get their emotions or their hair touched up too much. Then you want to have a flat-footed, heavy-breathing man with sandy whiskers, five kids and a building and loan mortgage ready as an understudy to take her desk. Now there was that widow lady that me and Andy Tucker engaged to help us in that little matrimonial agency scheme we floated out in Cairo.

"When you've got enough advertising capital—say a roll as big as the little end of a wagon tongue—there's money in matrimonial agencies. We had about $6,000 and we expected to double it in two months, which is about as long as a scheme like ours can be carried on without taking out a New Jersey charter.

"We fixed up an advertisement that read about like this:

'Charming widow, beautiful, home loving, 32 years, possessing $3,000 cash and owning valuable country property, would remarry. Would prefer a poor man

with affectionate disposition to one with means, as
she realizes that the solid virtues are oftenest to be
found in the humble walks of life. No objection to
elderly man or one of homely appearance if faithful
and true and competent to manage property and invest money with judgment. Address, with particulars,
                    Lonely,
        Care of Peters & Tucker, agents, Cairo, Ill.'

" 'So far, so pernicious,' says I, when we had finished the literary concoction. 'And now,' says I,
'where is the lady?'

"Andy gives me one of his looks of calm irritation.

" 'Jeff,' says he, 'I thought you had lost them ideas
of realism in your art. Why should there be a lady?
When they sell a lot of watered stock on Wall Street
would you expect to find a mermaid in it? What has
a matrimonial ad got to do with a lady?'

" 'Now listen,' says I. 'You know my rule, Andy,
that in all my illegitimate inroads against the legal
letter of the law the article sold must be existent, visible, producible. In that way and by a careful study of
city ordinances and train schedules I have kept out of
all trouble with the police that a five-dollar bill and a
cigar could not square. Now, to work this scheme
we've got to be able to produce bodily a charming
widow or its equivalent with or without the beauty,
hereditaments and appurtenances set forth in the cat-
alogue and writ of errors, or hereafter be held by a
justice of the peace.'

" 'Well,' says Andy, reconstructing his mind, 'maybe it would be safer in case the post office or the
peace commission should try to investigate our agency.
But where,' he says, 'could you hope to find a widow
who would waste time on a matrimonial scheme that
had no matrimony in it?'

"I told Andy that I thought I knew of the exact
party. An old friend of mine, Zeke Trotter, who used
to draw soda water and teeth in a tent show, had
made his wife a widow a year before by drinking some

dyspepsia cure of the old doctor's instead of the liniment that he always got boozed up on. I used to stop at their house often, and I thought we could get her to work with us.

" 'Twas only sixty miles to the little town where she lived, so I jumped out on the I.C. and finds her in the same cottage with the same sunflowers and roosters standing on the washtubs. Mrs. Trotter fitted our ad first rate except, maybe, for beauty and age and property valuation. But she looked feasible and praiseworthy to the eye, and it was a kindness to Zeke's memory to give her the job.

" 'Is this an honest deal you are putting on, Mr. Peters?' she asks me when I tell her what we want.

" 'Mrs. Trotter,' " says I, 'Andy Trotter and me have computed the calculation that 3,000 men in this broad and fair country will endeavor to secure your fair hand and ostensible money and property through our advertisement. Out of that number something like thirty hundred will expect to give you in exchange, if they should win you, the carcass of a lazy and mercenary loafer, a failure in life, a swindler and contemptible fortune seeker.

" 'Me and Andy,' says I, 'propose to teach these preyers upon society a lesson. It was with difficulty,' says I, 'that me and Andy could refrain from forming a corporation under the title of the Great Moral and Millennial Malevolent Matrimonial Agency. Does that satisfy you?'

" 'It does, Mr. Peters,' says she. 'I might have known you wouldn't have gone into anything that wasn't opprobrious. But what will my duties be? Do I have to reject personally these 3,000 ramscallions you speak of, or can I throw them out in bunches?'

" 'Your job, Mrs. Trotter,' says I, 'will be practically a cynosure. You will live at a quiet hotel and will have no work to do. Andy and I will attend to all the correspondence and business end of it.

" 'Of course,' says I, 'some of the more ardent and

impetuous suitors who can raise the railroad fare may come to Cairo to personally press their suit or whatever fraction of a suit they may be wearing. In that case you will be probably put to the inconvenience of kicking them out face to face. We will pay you $25 per week and hotel expenses.'

" 'Give me five minutes,' says Mrs. Trotter, 'to get my powder rag and leave the front door key with a neighbor and you can let my salary begin.'

"So I conveys Mrs. Trotter to Cairo and establishes her in a family hotel far enough away from mine and Andy's quarters to be unsuspicious and available, and I tell Andy.

" 'Great,' says Andy. 'And now that your conscience is appeased as to the tangibility and proximity of the bait, and leaving mutton aside, suppose we revenoo a noo fish.'

"So, we began to insert our advertisement in newspapers covering the country far and wide. One ad was all we used. We couldn't have used more without hiring so many clerks and marcelled paraphernalia that the sound of the gum chewing would have disturbed the Postmaster-General.

"We placed $2,000 in a bank to Mrs. Trotter's credit and gave her the book to show in case anybody might question the honesty and good faith of the agency. I knew Mrs. Trotter was square and reliable and it was safe to leave it in her name.

"With that one ad Andy and me put in twelve hours a day answering letters.

"About one hundred a day was what came in. I never knew there was so many large hearted but indigent men in the country who were willing to acquire a charming widow and assume the burden of investing her money.

"Most of them admitted that they ran principally to whiskers and lost jobs and were misunderstood by the world, but all of 'em were sure that they were so chock full of affection and manly qualities that the widow would be making the bargain of her life to get 'em.

"Every applicant got a reply from Peters & Tucker informing him that the widow had been deeply impressed by his straightforward and interesting letter and requesting them to write again stating more particulars; and enclosing photograph if convenient. Peters & Tucker also informed the applicant that their fee for handing over the second letter to their fair client would be $2, enclosed therewith.

"There you see the simple beauty of the scheme. About 90 percent of them domestic foreign noblemen raised the price somehow and sent it in. That was all there was to it. Except that me and Andy complained an amount about being put to the trouble of slicing open them envelopes, and taking the money out.

"Some few clients called in person. We sent 'em to Mrs. Trotter and she did the rest; except for three or four who came back to strike us for carfare. After the letters began to get in from the r.f.d. districts Andy and me were taking in about $200 a day.

"One afternoon when we were busiest and I was stuffing the two and ones into cigar boxes and Andy was whistling 'No Wedding Bells for Her' a small, slick man drops in and runs his eye over the walls like he was on the trail of a lost Gainesborough painting or two. As soon as I saw him I felt a glow of pride, because we were running our business on the level.

" 'I see you have quite a large mail today,' says the man.

"I reached and got my hat.

" 'Come on,' says I. 'We've been expecting you. I'll show you the goods. How was Teddy when you left Washington?"

"I took him down to the Riverview Hotel and had him shake hands with Mrs. Trotter. Then I showed him her bank book with the $2,000 to her credit.

" 'It seems to be all right,' says the Secret Service.

" 'It is,' says I. 'And if you're not a married man I'll

leave you to talk a while with the lady. We won't mention the two dollars.'

" 'Thanks,' says he. 'If I wasn't, I might. Good day, Mr. Peters.'

"Toward the end of three months we had taken in something over $5,000, and we saw it was time to quit. We had a good many complaints made to us; and Mrs. Trotter seemed to be tired of the job. A good many suitors had been calling to see her, and she didn't seem to like that.

"So we decides to pull out, and I goes down to Mrs Trotter's hotel to pay her last week's salary and say farewell and get her check for $2,000.

"When I get there I found her crying like a kid that don't want to go to school.

" 'Now, now,' says I, 'what's it all about? Somebody sassed you or you getting homesick?'

" 'No, Mr. Peters,' says she. 'I'll tell you. You was always a friend of Zeke's, and I don't mind. Mr. Peters, I'm in love. I just love a man so hard I can't bear not to get him. He's just the ideal I've always had in mind.'

" 'Then take him,' says I. 'That is, if it's a mutual case. Does he return the sentiment according to the specifications and painfulness you have described?'

" 'He does,' says she. 'But he's one of the gentlemen that's been coming to see me about the advertisement and he won't marry me unless I give him the $2,000. His name is William Wilkinson.' And then she goes off again in the agitations and hysterics of romance.

" 'Mrs. Trotter,' says I, 'there's no man more sympathizing with a woman's affections than I am. Besides, you was once a life partner of one of my best friends. If it was left to me I'd say take this $2,000 and the man of your choice and be happy.

" 'We could afford to do that, because we have cleaned up over $5,000 from these suckers that wanted to marry you. But,' says I, 'Andy Tucker is to be consulted.'

"I goes back to our hotel and lays the case before Andy.

" 'I was expecting something like this all the time,' says Andy. 'You can't trust a woman to stick by you in any scheme that involves her emotions and preferences.'

" 'It's a sad thing, Andy,' says I, 'to think that we've been the cause of the breaking of a woman's heart.'

" 'It is,' says Andy, 'and I tell you what I'm willing to do, Jeff. You've always been a man of a soft and generous disposition. Perhaps I've been too hard and worldly and suspicious. For once I'll meet you half way. Go to Mrs. Trotter and tell her to draw the $2,000 from the bank and give it to this man she's infatuated with and be happy.'

"I jumps and shakes Andy's hand for five minutes, and then I goes back to Mrs. Trotter and tells her, and she cries as hard for joy as she did for sorrow.

"Two days afterward me and Andy packed to go.

" 'Wouldn't you like to go down and meet Mrs. Trotter once before we leave?' I asks him. 'She'd like mightily to know you and express her encomiums and gratitude.'

" 'Why, I guess not,' says Andy. 'I guess we'd better hurry and catch that train.'

"I was strapping our capital around me in a memory belt like we always carried it, when Andy pulls a roll of large bills out of his pocket and asks me to put 'em with the rest.

" 'What's this?' says I.

" 'It's Mrs. Trotter's two thousand,' says Andy.

" 'How do you come to have it?' I asks.

" 'She gave it to me,' says Andy. 'I've been calling on her three evenings a week for more than a month.'

" 'Then you are William Wilkinson?' says I.

" 'I was,' says Andy."

The Wife

BY WASHINGTON IRVING

▭ ▭ ▭

The treasures of the deep are not so precious
As are the conceal'd comforts of a man
Locked up in woman's love. I scent the air
Of blessings, when I come but near the house.
What a delicious breath marriage sends forth . . .
The violet bed's not sweeter.

MIDDLETON

I have often had the occasion to remark the fortitude with which women sustain the most over-
whelming reverses of fortune. Those disasters which
break down the spirit of a man, and prostrate him in
the dust, seem to call forth all energies of the softer
sex, and give such intrepidity and elevation to their
character, that at times it approaches to sublimity.
Nothing can be more touching than to behold a soft
and tender female, who had been all weakness and de-
pendence, and alive to every trivial roughness, while
treading the prosperous paths of life, suddenly rising
in mental force to be the comforter and support of
her husband under misfortune, and abiding, with un-
shrinking firmness, the bitterest blasts of adversity.

As the vine, which has long twined its graceful
foliage about the oak, and been lifted by it into sunshine, will, when the hardy plant is rifted by the thun-
derbolt, cling round it with its caressing tendrils and
bind up its shattered boughs, so is it beautifully ordered
by Providence, that woman, who is the mere dependent

and ornament of man in his happier hours, should be his stay and solace when smitten with sudden calamity; winding herself into the rugged recesses of his nature, tenderly supporting the drooping head, and binding up the broken heart.

I was once congratulating a friend, who had around him a blooming family, knit together in the strongest affection. "I can wish you no better lot," said he with enthusiasm, "than to have a wife and children. If you are prosperous, there they are to share your prosperity; if otherwise, there they are to comfort you." And indeed, I have observed that a married man falling into misfortune is more apt to retrieve his situation in the world than a single one; partly because he is more stimulated to exertion by the necessities of the helpless and beloved beings who depend upon him for subsistence; but chiefly because his spirits are soothed and relieved by domestic endearments, and his self-respect kept alive by finding that, though all abroad is darkness and humiliation, yet there is still a little world of love at home, of which he is the monarch. Whereas a single man is apt to run to waste and self-neglect; to fancy himself lonely and abandoned, and his heart to fall to ruin like some deserted mansion, for want of an inhabitant.

These observations call to mind a little domestic story, of which I was once a witness. My intimate friend, Leslie, had married a beautiful and accomplished girl, who had been brought up in the midst of fashionable life. She had, it is true, no fortune, but that of my friend was ample; and he delighted in the anticipation of indulging her in every elegant pursuit, and administering to those delicate tastes and fancies that spread a kind of witchery about the sex.—"Her life," said he, "shall be like a fairy tale."

The very difference in their characters produced a harmonious combination: he was of a romantic and somewhat serious cast; she was all life and gladness. I have often noticed the mute rapture with which he would gaze upon her in company, of which her sprightly powers made her the delight; and how, in the midst of applause, her eyes would still turn to him, as if there alone she sought favor and acceptance. When leaning on his arm, her slender form contrasted finely with his tall manly person. The fond confiding air with which she looked up at him seemed to call forth a flush of triumphant pride and cherishing tenderness, as if he doted on his lovely burden for its very helplessness. Never did a couple set forward on the flowery path of early and well-suited marriage with a fairer prospect of felicity.

It was the misfortune of my friend, however, to have embarked his property in large speculations; and he had not been married many months when, by a succession of sudden disasters, it was swept from him, and he found himself reduced almost to penury. For a time he kept his situation to himself, and went about with a haggard countenance and a breaking heart. His life was but a protracted agony; and what rendered it more insupportable was the necessity of keeping up a smile in the presence of his wife; for he could not bring himself to overwhelm her with the news. She saw, however, with the quick eye of affection, that all was not well with him. She marked his altered looks and stifled sighs, and was not to be deceived by his sickly and vapid attempts at cheerfulness. She tasked all her sprightly powers and tender blandishments to win him back to happiness; but she only drove the arrow deeper into his soul. The more he saw cause to love her, the more torturing was the thought that he was soon to make her wretched. A little while, thought he, and the smile will vanish from that cheek —the song will die away from those lips—the lustre of those eyes will be quenched with sorrow; and the happy heart, which now beats lightly in that bosom, will be weighted down like mine by the cares and miseries of the world.

At length he came to me one day, and related his

whole situation in a tone of the deepest despair. When I heard him through I inquired, "Does your wife know all this?"—At the question he burst into an agony of tears. "For God's sake!" cried he, "if you have any pity on me, don't mention my wife; it is the thought of her that drives me almost to madness!"

"And why not?" said I. "She must know it sooner or later: you cannot keep it long from her, and the intelligence may break upon her in a more startling manner, than if imparted by yourself; for the accents of those we love soften the harshest tidings. Besides, you are depriving yourself of the comforts of her sympathy; and not merely that, but also endangering the only bond that can keep hearts together—an unreserved community of thought and feeling. She will soon perceive that something is secretly preying upon your mind; and true love will not brook reserve; it feels under-valued and outraged, when even the sorrows of those it loves are concealed from it."

"Oh, but my friend! to think what a blow I am to give to all her future prospects—how I am to strike her very soul to the earth by telling her that her husband is a beggar; that she is to forego all the elegancies of life—all the pleasures of society—to shrink with me into indigence and obscurity! To tell her that I have dragged her down from the sphere in which she might have continued to move in constant brightness—the light of every eye—the admiration of every heart!—How can she bear poverty? she has been brought up in all the refinements of opulence. How can she bear neglect? she has been the idol of society. Oh! it will break her heart—it will break her heart!—"

I saw his grief was eloquent, and I let it have its flow; for sorrow relieves itself by words. When his paroxysm had subsided, and he had relapsed into moody silence, I resumed the subject gently, and urged him to break his situation at once to his wife. He shook his head mournfully, but positively.

"But how are you going to keep it from her? It is

necessary she should know it, that you may take the steps proper to the alteration of your circumstances. You must change your style of living—nay," observing a pang to pass across his countenance, "don't let that afflict you. I am sure you have never placed your happiness in outward show—you have yet friends, warm friends, who will not think the worse of you for being less splendidly lodged; and surely it does not require a palace to be happy with Mary—"

"I could be happy with her," cried he, convulsively, "in a hovel!—I could go down with her into poverty and the dust!—I could—I could—God bless her!— God bless her!" cried he, bursting into a transport of grief and tenderness.

"And believe me, my friend," I said, stepping up and grasping him warmly by the hand, "believe me she can be the same with you. Ay, more: it will be a source of pride and triumph to her—it will call forth all the latent energies and fervent sympathies of her nature; for she will rejoice to prove that she loves you for yourself. There is in every true woman's heart a spark of heavenly fire, which lies dormant in the broad daylight of prosperity; but which kindles up and beams and blazes in the dark hour of adversity. No man knows what the wife of his bosom is—no man knows what a ministering angel she is—unless he has gone with her through the fiery trials of this world."

There was something in the earnestness of my manner, and the figurative style of my language, that caught the excited imagination of Leslie. I knew the auditor I had to deal with; and following up the impression I had made, I finished by persuading him to go home and unburden his sad heart to his wife.

I must confess, notwithstanding all I had said, I felt some little solicitude for the result. Who can calculate on the fortitude of one whose life has been a round of pleasures? Her gay spirits might revolt at the dark downward path of low humility suddenly pointed out before her, and might cling to the sunny regions in which they had hitherto revelled. Besides, ruin in fashionable life is accompanied by so many galling mortifications, to which in other ranks it is a stranger.—In short, I could not meet Leslie the next morning without trepidation. He had made the disclosure.

"And how did she bear it?"

"Like an angel! It seemed rather to be a relief to her mind, for she threw her arms round my neck, and asked if this was all that had lately made me unhappy.—But, poor girl," added he, "she cannot realize the change we must undergo. She has no idea of poverty but in the abstract; she has only read of it in poetry, where it is allied to love. She feels as yet no privation; she suffers no loss of accustomed conveniences nor elegancies. When we come practically to experience its sordid cares, its paltry wants, its petty humiliations—then will be the real trial."

"But," said I, "now that you have got over the severest task, that of breaking it to her, the sooner you let the world into the secret the better. The disclosure may be mortifying; but then it is a single misery and soon over: whereas you otherwise suffer it in anticipation, every hour of the day. It is not poverty so much as pretence, that harasses a ruined man—the struggle between a proud mind and an empty purse—the keeping up a hollow show that must soon come to an end. Have the courage to appear poor and you disarm poverty of its sharpest sting." On this point I found Leslie perfectly prepared. He had no false pride himself, and as to his wife, she was only anxious to conform to their altered fortunes.

Some days afterwards he called upon me in the evening. He had disposed of his dwelling house and taken a small cottage in the country, a few miles from town. He had been busied all day in sending out furniture. The new establishment required few articles, and those of the simplest kind. All the splendid furniture of his late residence had been sold, excepting his wife's harp. That, he said, was too closely associated with the idea of herself; it belonged to the little story of their loves; for some of the sweetest moments of their courtship were those when he had leaned over that instrument and listened to the melting tones of her voice. I could not but smile at this instance of romantic gallantry in a doting husband.

He was now going out to the cottage, where his wife had been all day superintending its arrangements. My feelings had become strongly interested in the progress of this family story, and, as it was a fine evening, I offered to accompany him.

He was wearied with the fatigues of the day, and as he walked out, fell into a fit of gloomy musing.

"Poor Mary!" at length broke, with a heavy sigh, from his lips.

"And what of her?" asked I: "has anything happened to her?"

"What," said he, darting an impatient glance, "is it nothing to be reduced to this paltry situation—to be caged in a miserable cottage—to be obliged to toil almost in the menial concerns of her wretched habitation?"

"Has she then repined at the change?"

"Repined! she has been nothing but sweetness and good humor. Indeed, she seems in better spirits than I have ever known her; she has been to me all love, and tenderness, and comfort!"

"Admirable girl!" exclaimed I. "You call yourself poor, my friend; you never were so rich—you never knew the boundless treasures of excellence you possess in that woman."

"Oh! but, my friend, if this first meeting at the cottage were over, I think I could then be comfortable. But this is her first day of real experience; she has been introduced into a humble dwelling—she has been employed all day in arranging its miserable equipments—she has, for the first time, known the fatigues of domestic employment—she has, for the first time, looked round her on a home destitute of every-thing elegant,—almost of everything convenient; and may now be sitting down, exhausted and spiritless, brooding over a prospect of future poverty."

There was a degree of probability in this picture that I could not gainsay, so we walked on in silence.

After turning from the main road up a narrow lane, so thickly shaded with forest trees as to give it a com-plete air of seclusion, we came in sight of the cot-tage. It was humble enough in its appearance, for the most pastoral poet; and yet it had a pleasing rural look. A wild vine had overrun one end in a profusion of foliage; a few trees threw their branches gracefully over it; and I observed several pots of flowers taste-fully disposed about the door and on the grassplot in front. A small wicket gate opened upon a footpath that wound through some shrubbery to the door. Just as we approached, we heard the sound of music— Leslie grasped my arm; we paused and listened. It was Mary's voice singing, in a style of the most touch-ing simplicity, a little air of which her husband was peculiarly fond.

I felt Leslie's hand tremble on my arm. He stepped forward to hear more distinctly. His step made a noise on the gravel walk. A bright beautiful face glanced out at the window and vanished—a light footstep was heard—and Mary came tripping forth to greet us: she was in a pretty rural dress of white; a few wild flowers were twisted in her fine hair; a fresh bloom was on her cheek; her whole countenance beamed with smiles—I had never seen her look so lovely.

"My dear George," cried she, "I am so glad you are come! I have been watching and watching for you; and running down the lane, and looking out for you. I've set out a table under a beautiful tree behind the cot-tage; and I've been gathering some of the most de-licious strawberries for I know you are fond of them—and we have such excellent cream—and everything is so sweet and still here—Oh!" said she, putting her arm within his, and looking up brightly in his face, "Oh, we shall be so happy!"

Poor Leslie was overcome. He caught her to his bosom—he folded his arms round her—he kissed her again and again—he could not speak, but the tears gushed into his eyes; and he has often assured me, that though the world has since gone prosperously with him, and his life has, indeed, been a happy one, yet never has he experienced a moment of more exquisite felicity.

If Not Still Higher

BY ISAAC LOEB PEREZ

And every morning during Slichos, the penitential
days between Rosh Hashonah and Yom Kippur, the
Rebbe of Nemirov would vanish, disappear!

He was not to be seen anywhere; not in shull, not in
either of the two houses-of-prayer, not in any minyan,
and certainly not at home. The house was constantly
open. Everyone who pleased could go in and out. Of
course, no one would rob the Rebbe, but there wasn't
a living soul in the house.

Where can the Rebbe be?

Where should he be? In Heaven, most likely.
Doesn't a Rebbe have enough to do in the time between the High Holy Days? Jews, no evil befall them,
are in need of a livelihood, peace, health, happy
matches for their children; they want to be good and
pious, and sins are so numerous, and Satan with his
thousand eyes peers from one end of the world to
the other; he sees all, spreads rumors and tells tales
. . . and—who should be of service if not the Rebbe?

That's what the people believed.

However, once a Litvak came to town; he laughed
in scorn! You know the Litvaks—they want to see for
themselves! This Litvak points to a definite section of
the gemara as if to gouge out our eyes: even Moses
himself, he proves, could not get into Heaven in his
lifetime. Well, argue with a Litvak!

Well then, where *does* the Rebbe go?

"I should worry!" he answers and shrugs his shoulders; and in the midst of the argument (there's a Litvak for you!) he determines to find out for himself.

That very evening, right after prayers, the Litvak steals into the Rebbe's room, creeps under the Rebbe's bed and stretches out. He must spend the night there to see where the Rebbe disappears, what he does during Slichos.

Another might have dozed off and slept; a Litvak loses no time: he memorized a whole portion of gemara by heart.

At dawn he hears a knocking for Slichos prayers.

The Rebbe has been awake for some time; the Litvak heard the Rebbe groaning for at least an hour.

He who has heard the Rebbe of Nemirov groan knows what sorrows for all Israel, what sufferings are contained in each groan. . . . The soul would expire at the sound of those groans. But the heart of a Litvak is made of iron, so he listens and continues to lie there! The Rebbe, too, continues to rest—the Rebbe, long life to him—in bed, and the Litvak under it.

After a while the Litvak hears the beds in the house begin to creak . . . as people leap out of them; he hears a murmur of talk, sounds of water poured on the finger-nails, of doors opening and shutting. . . . Later, people leave the house and once more it turns quiet and dark; a ray of moonlight barely shines through the shutter. . . .

The Litvak confessed that when he remained alone with the Rebbe, he became terrified. His skin almost shrank for fright. The roots of his ear-locks stabbed his temples like needles.

No trifle this—alone in the house with the Rebbe at dawn of a Slichos-day.

But, a Litvak is a stubborn fellow. He trembled like a leaf and continued to lie there.

Finally, the Rebbe, long life to him, gets up. . . .

First he does what is proper for Jews to do. . . .

Then he goes to the wardrobe and takes out a bundle.

. . . Peasant clothing: linen trousers, large boots, a fur coat, a great fur hat, and a broad, long leather belt studded with brass nails.

The Rebbe puts them on.

Out of the pocket of the fur coat dangles an end of thick rope . . . a peasant's rope.

The Rebbe walks out; the Litvak—after him!

On his way, the Rebbe steps into the kitchen, stoops and, from under a bed, takes an axe, sticks it into the belt and leaves the house.

The Litvak trembles but does not stop following.

A faint, mid-holiday hush trembles over the quiet streets. Frequently a cry breaks forth from a minyan at prayer, or an invalid's groan from some window. . . . The Rebbe hurries on, keeping to the side of the street, in the shadows of the houses . . . he glides from one house to the next, the Litvak after him. . . .

And the Litvak becomes aware that his heart-beat merges with the beat of the Rebbe's heavy steps. But he continues and arrives on the outskirts of the town with the Rebbe.

Beyond the town there is a little woods.

The Rebbe, long life to him, goes into the woods. He walks thirty or forty paces and stops beside a small tree, and the Litvak is amazed and frightened as he sees the Rebbe remove the axe from his belt and began to chop the tree down.

He sees the Rebbe strike again and again; he hears the tree groan and snap. The little tree falls and the Rebbe cuts it into logs . . . the logs into splinters; then, with the rope from his pocket, he ties the splinters into a bundle of fire-wood, swings the bundle onto his shoulders, shoves the axe into the belt, walks out of the wood and returns to the town.

In a back alley he stops at a poor, broken-down house and knocks at a small window.

"Who is it?" a frightened voice calls from the house. The Litvak can tell that it is the voice of an old Jewess, of a sick Jewess.

"I," the Rebbe answers, speaking in peasant speech.

"Who is it?" the voice in the house asks again. And the Rebbe, again speaking in Little-Russian, says: "Vassil."

"What Vassil? And what do you want, Vassil?"

"Firewood," the disguised peasant says, "I have fire-wood to sell! Very cheap. Wood for next to nothing."

And without waiting for an answer, he enters the house.

The Litvak also steals in and by the gray light of morning sees a shabby room with broken, poor house-hold goods. . . . In bed lies a sick Jewess, wrapped in rags. She speaks in a bitter tone:

"Who can buy? With what shall I buy? Where do I, a poor widow, have the money?"

"I will trust you!" the disguised peasant answers, "it comes to only six groschen!"

"And with what will I pay you?" the poor woman groans.

"Foolish creature," the Rebbe says rebukingly. "Just think, you are a poor, sick woman and I give you this bundle of wood on trust; I have faith in your paying for it; and you, who have such a mighty and great God, have no faith in Him! You do not trust Him for even a silly six groschen's worth of wood!"

"And who will kindle my fire?" the widow groans. "Do I have the strength to get up? And my son stayed over at his work."

"I will also light the stove for you," says the Rebbe.

And laying the wood in the stove, the Rebbe groans as he recites the first section of penitential prayers.

And when he lighted the fire and the wood burned merrily, he said more cheerfully the second section of penitential prayers. . . .

He said the third section when the fire had burned itself out, and he shut the doors of the stove. . . .

The Litvak who saw all this remained a disciple of the Rebbe of Nemirov.

And after that when any disciple would relate that

the Rebbe of Nemirov at Slichos time arose every morning and flew up to heaven, the Litvak would not laugh, but would add quietly:

"If not still higher!"

The Wild Duck's Nest

BY MICHAEL MC LAVERTY

The sun was setting, spilling gold light on the low western hills of Rathlin Island. A small boy walked jauntily along a hoof-printed path that wriggled between the folds of these hills and opened out into a crater-like valley on the cliff-top. Presently he stopped as if remembering something, then suddenly he left the path and began running up one of the hills. When he reached the top he was out of breath and stood watching streaks of light radiating from golden-edged clouds, the scene reminding him of a picture he had seen of the Transfiguration. A short distance below him was the cow standing at the edge of a reedy lake. Colm ran down to meet her waving his stick in the air, and the wind rumbling in his ears made him give an exultant whoop which splashed upon the hills in a shower of echoed sound. A flock of gulls lying on the short grass near the lake rose up languidly, drifting like blown snowflakes over the rim of the cliff.

The lake faced west and was fed by a stream, the drainings of the semi-circling hills. One side was open to the winds from the sea and in winter a little outlet trickled over the cliffs making a black vein in their gray sides. The boy lifted stones and began throwing them into the lake, weaving web after web on its calm surface. Then he skimmed the water with flat stones, some of them jumping the surface and coming to rest on the other side. He was delighted with himself and after listening to his echoing shouts of delight he ran to fetch his cow. Gently he tapped her on the side and reluctantly she went towards the brown-mudded path that led out of the valley. The boy was about to throw a final stone into the lake when a bird flew low over his head, its neck astrain, and its orange-colored legs clear in the soft light. It was a wild duck. It circled the lake twice, thrice, coming lower each time and then with a nervous flapping of wings it skidded along the surface, its legs breaking the water into a series of silvery arcs. Its wings closed, it lit silently, gave a slight shiver, and began pecking indifferently at the water.

Colm, with dilated eyes, eagerly watched it making for the farther end of the lake. It meandered between tall bulrushes, its body black and solid as stone against the graying water. Then as if it had sunk it was gone. The boy ran stealthily along the bank looking away from the lake, pretending indifference. When he came opposite to where he had last seen the bird he stopped and peered through the sighing reeds whose shadows streaked the water in a maze of black strokes. In front of him was a soddy islet guarded by the spears of sedge and separated from the bank by a narrow channel of water. The water wasn't too deep—he could wade across with care.

Rolling up his short trousers he began to wade, his arms outstretched, and his legs brown in the mountain water. As he drew near the islet, his feet sank in the cold mud and bubbles winked up at him. He went more carefully and nervously. Then one trouser leg fell and dipped into the water; the boy dropped his hands to roll it up, he unbalanced, made a splashing sound, and the bird arose with a squawk and whirred away over the cliffs. For a moment the boy stood frightened. Then he clambered on to the wet-soaked sod of land, which was spattered with sea gulls' feathers and bits of wind-blown rushes.

Into each hummock he looked, pulling back the long

grass. At last he came on the nest, facing seawards. Two flat rocks dimpled the face of the water and between them was a neck of land matted with coarse grass containing the nest. It was untidily built of dried rushes, straw and feathers, and in it lay one solitary egg. Colm was delighted. He looked around and saw no one. The nest was his. He lifted the egg, smooth and green as the sky, with a faint tinge of yellow like the reflected light from a buttercup; and then he felt he had done wrong. He put it back. He knew he shouldn't have touched it and he wondered would the bird forsake the nest. A vague sadness stole over him and he felt in his heart he had sinned. Carefully smoothing out his footprints he hurriedly left the islet and ran after his cow. The sun had now set and the cold shiver of evening enveloped him, chilling his body and saddening his mind.

In the morning he was up and away to school. He took the grass rut that edged the road for it was softer on the bare feet. His house was the last on the western headland and after a mile or so he was joined by Paddy McFall; both boys, dressed in similar hand-knitted blue jerseys and gray trousers, carried homemade school bags. Colm was full of the nest and as soon as he joined his companion he said eagerly: "Paddy, I've a nest—a wild duck's with one egg."

"And how do you know it's a wild duck's?" asked Paddy, slightly jealous.

"Sure I saw her with my own two eyes, her brown speckled back with a crow's patch on it, and her yellow legs—"

"Where is it?" interrupted Paddy in a challenging tone.

"I'm not going to tell you, for you'd rob it!"

"Aach! I suppose it's a tame duck's you have or maybe an old gull's."

Colm put out his tongue at him. "A lot you know!" he said, "for a gull's egg has spots and this one is greenish-white, for I had it in my hand."

And then the words he didn't want to hear rushed from Paddy in a mocking chant, "You had it in your hand! . . . She'll forsake it! She'll forsake it! She'll forsake it!" he said, skipping along the road before him.

Colm felt as if he would choke or cry with vexation.

His mind told him that Paddy was right, but somehow he couldn't give in to it and he replied: "She'll not forsake it! She'll not. I know she'll not!"

But in school his faith wavered. Through the windows he could see moving sheets of rain—rain that dribbled down the panes filling his mind with thoughts of the lake creased and chilled by wind; the nest sodden and black with wetness; and the egg cold as a cave stone. He shivered from the thoughts and fidgeted with the inkwell cover, sliding it backwards and forwards mechanically. The mischievous look had gone from his eyes and the school day dragged on interminably. But at last they were out in the rain, Colm rushing home as fast as he could.

He was no time at all at his dinner of potatoes and salted fish until he was out in the valley now smoky with drifts of slanting rain. Opposite the islet he entered the water. The wind was blowing into his face, rustling noisily the rushes heavy with the dust of rain. A moss-cheeper, swaying on a reed like a mouse, filled the air with light cries of loneliness.

The boy reached the islet, his heart thumping with excitement, wondering did the bird forsake. He went slowly, quietly, on to the strip of land that led to the nest. He rose on his toes, looking over the ledge to see if he could see her. And then every muscle tautened. She was on, her shoulders hunched up, and her bill lying on her breast as if she were asleep. Colm's heart hammered wildly in his ears. She hadn't forsaken. He was about to turn stealthily away. Something happened. The bird moved, her neck straightened, twitching nervously from side to side. The boy's head swam with lightness. He stood transfixed. The wild duck with a panicky flapping, rose heavily, and flew off to-

wards the sea. . . . A guilty silence enveloped the boy.
. . . He turned to go away, hesitated, and glanced back
at the bare nest; it'd be no harm to have a look. Tim-
idly he approached it; standing straight, and gazing
over the edge. There in the nest lay two eggs. He
drew in his breath with delight, splashed quickly from
the island, and ran off whistling in the rain.

How the Devil Lost His Poncho

BY RICARDO PALMA

◫ ◫ ◫

Once, when Our Lord was traveling about the world upon His gentle little donkey, restoring sight to the blind and recovering the use of their limbs to the lame, He came into a region where there was nothing at all but sand. Here and there was a rustling, slender palm under whose shade Gentle Jesus would stop with His disciples, who would fill their sacks with dates.

As eternal as the Lord Himself seemed that desert, with neither beginning nor end. The travelers, heavy-hearted, prepared to spend the night with only a starry sky for shelter, when, picked out by the last ray of the setting sun, the silhouette of a belfry showed upon the horizon.

Lord Jesus, shading His eyes to see better, said: "I see a town over there. Peter, you know all about geography. Could you tell me what city that is?"

St. Peter grinned at the compliment.

"Master, that is the city of Ica."

"Well, then. Let us move along."

The donkeys joggled along briskly, and they all soon reached town. Jesus, just before they entered, gently reminded Peter that he must not lose his temper. "You're always getting us into trouble with your temper," said Our Lord. "Please try to keep it under control."

The people of the city rolled out the welcome mat for these illustrious visitors. Even though the little party was anxious to be on its way, the townsfolk made

90

everything so pleasant that a week had passed before you could whistle. During that week the city of Ica seemed like the alcove of Paradise. Doctors and dentists sat idly in their offices, and the druggists made up no prescriptions. Not a complaint was registered before the advocates. There was not even a cross word between husband or wife, nor any—miracle of miracles! —nor any malice expressed by mothers- and sisters-in-law.

How long this idyllic existence might have gone on nobody knows, for on the eighth day Our Lord received a message calling Him to return to Jerusalem to stand between Mary Magdalene and the unfriendly Samaritan women. Rather than bother the hospitable folk of Ica with long-winded excuses and explanations, the Gentle Traveler decided to leave suddenly, during the night, with His companions.

Early the next morning, then, when the city council called to give a special morning concert, they found their guests gone.

But after He and His party had gone several miles from the city, the Lord turned and blessed the little town of Ica in the name of the Father, the Son, and the Holy Ghost.

Naturally such a succession of events could not remain out of the newspapers. The Devil, therefore, received the news by the earliest mail. He gnashed his teeth with chagrin and swore that no one could steal a march on him. Calling together the chief of his demons he had them disguise themselves as disciples. The art of make-up and disguise is certainly close to the heart of the Horned One. So, putting on high boots and ponchos, he and his party started on their journey.

The citizens of Ica, seeing the travelers in the distance, rushed out to greet them, hoping this time that The Lord and His companions would remain with them forever.

Up to this time, of course, there had been happiness

and content in Ica such as existed nowhere else. The citizens paid their taxes without complaint, let the politicians run politics, and regarded helping their neighbors as the most important thing in life.

Needless to say this bliss made the Devil quiver with rage, and he determined to upset the apple cart at the first opportunity.

Just at the time the Devil arrived, a marriage was about to take place between a young man and a young girl made for each other as ewe for ram; here was a perfect match.

Satan waited his time, as he always does, and when the toasts began to go down the thirsty gullets, the liquor produced not the friendly elevation of spirits that banquets should foster, but a coarse, indecent frenzy. Insulting remarks were hurled at the bride, and several women made advances towards the handsome groom.

And things went further than this. For all the doctors and dentists and druggists and advocates began to do a rushing business. Family squabbles flourished; mothers-in-law seemed to make up for time lost; wives remembered it was their duty and prerogative to whine and cry for new dresses and expensive jewelry. To top it all, the city council decided it was time to levy new taxes. It was obvious, wasn't it, that only the Devil could be at the bottom of this?

In the meantime the poor bride, trying desperately to stop the fighting and brawling, kept muttering, "It must be the Devil gotten into them. That's what it must be."

She rushed to the Evil One in disguise and tugged at his poncho.

"Oh, Lord," she cried. "They are all going to kill one another."

"What do I care?" sneered old Cloven Hoof. "It's no concern of mine. The worse it gets, the better I like it."

The poor girl, amazed, berated him.

"What a heart Your Excellency has. It's like a stone.

You must be the Devil himself." And she made the sign of the cross with her fingers.

No sooner had the Evil One seen her gesture than he tried to race from the scene. But she had a strong hold on his poncho, and he had to duck his head through the opening, leaving the cape in the girl's hand.

The Devil's party disappeared in a puff, but, since then, every once in a while, old Satan comes back to Ica, searching for his poncho. Whenever this happens the liquor starts flowing, of course, and things get really lively all over again.

The Standard of Living

BY DOROTHY PARKER

Annabel and Midge came out of the tea room with the arrogant slow gait of the leisured, for their Saturday afternoon stretched ahead of them. They had lunched, as was their wont, on sugar, starches, oils, and butter-fats. Usually they ate sandwiches of spongy new white bread greased with butter and mayonnaise; they ate thick wedges of cake lying wet beneath ice cream and whipped cream and melted chocolate gritty with nuts. As alternates, they ate patties, sweating beads of inferior oil, containing bits of bland meat bogged in pale, stiffening sauce; they ate pastries, limber under rigid icing, filled with an indeterminate yellow sweet stuff, not still solid, not yet liquid, like salve that has been left in the sun. They chose no other sort of food, nor did they consider it. And their skin was like the petals of wood anemones, and their bellies were as flat and their flanks as lean as those of young Indian braves.

Annabel and Midge had been best friends almost from the day that Midge had found a job as stenographer with the firm that employed Annabel. By now, Annabel, two years longer in the stenographic department, had worked up to the wages of eighteen dollars and fifty cents a week; Midge was still at sixteen dollars. Each girl lived at home with her family and paid half her salary to its support.

The girls sat side by side at their desks, they lunched together every noon, together they set out for home

at the end of the day's work. Many of their evenings
and most of their Sundays were passed in each other's
company. Often they were joined by two young men,
but there was no steadiness to any such quartet; the
two young men would give place, unlamented, to two
other young men, and lament would have been inap-
propriate, really, since the newcomers were scarcely
distinguishable from their predecessors. Invariably the
girls spent the fine idle hours of their hot-weather
Saturday afternoons together. Constant use had not
worn ragged the fabric of their friendship.

They looked alike, though the resemblance did not
lie in their features. It was in the shape of their bodies,
their movements, their style, and their adornments.
Annabel and Midge did, and completely, all that young
office workers are besought not to do. They painted
their lips and their nails, they darkened their lashes
and lightened their hair, and scent seemed to shim-
mer from them. They wore thin, bright dresses, tight
over their breasts and high on their legs, and tilted
slippers, fancifully strapped. They looked conspicuous
and cheap and charming.

Now, as they walked across to Fifth Avenue with
their skirts swirled by the hot wind, they received audible admiration. Young men grouped lethargically about
newsstands awarded them murmurs, exclamations,
even—the ultimate tribute—whistles. Annabel and
Midge passed without the condescension of hurrying
their pace; they held their heads higher and set their
feet with exquisite precision, as if they stepped over
the necks of peasants.

Always the girls went to walk on Fifth Avenue on
their free afternoons, for it was the ideal ground for
their favorite game. The game could be played anywhere, and indeed, was, but the great shop windows
stimulated the two players to their best form.

Annabel had invented the game; or rather she had
evolved it from an old one. Basically, it was no more
than the ancient sport of what-would-you-do-if-you-had

a-million-dollars? But Annabel had drawn a new set of rules for it, had narrowed it, pointed it, made it stricter. Like all games, it was the more absorbing for being more difficult.

Annabel's version went like this: You must suppose that somebody dies and leaves you a million dollars, cool. But there is a condition to the bequest. It is stated in the will that you must spend every nickel of the money on yourself.

There lay the hazard of the game. If, when playing it, you forgot and listed among your expenditures the rental of a new apartment for your family, for example, you lost your turn to the other player. It was astonishing how many—and some of them among the experts, too—would forfeit all their innings by such slips.

It was essential, of course, that it be played in passionate seriousness. Each purchase must be carefully considered and, if necessary, supported by argument. There was no zest to playing it wildly. Once Annabel had introduced the game to Sylvia, another girl who worked in the office. She explained the rules to Sylvia and then offered her the gambit "What would be the first thing you'd do?" Sylvia had not shown the decency of even a second of hesitation. "Well," she said, "the first thing I'd do, I'd go out and hire somebody to shoot Mrs. Gary Cooper, and then . . ." So it is to be seen that she was no fun.

But Annabel and Midge were surely born to be comrades, for Midge played the game like a master from the moment she learned it. It was she who added the touches that made the whole thing cozier. According to Midge's innovations, the eccentric who died and left you the money was not anybody you loved, or, for the matter of that, anybody you even knew. It was somebody who had seen you somewhere and had thought, "That girl ought to have lots of nice things. I'm going to leave her a million dollars when I die." And the death was to be neither untimely nor painful.

Your benefactor, full of years and comfortably ready to depart, was to slip softly away during sleep and go right to heaven. These embroideries permitted Annabel and Midge to play their game in the luxury of peaceful consciences.

Midge played with a seriousness that was not only proper but extreme. The single strain on the girls' friendship had followed an announcement once made by Annabel that the first thing she would buy with her million dollars would be a silver-fox coat. It was as if she had struck Midge across the mouth. When Midge recovered her breath, she cried that she couldn't imagine how Annabel could do such a thing—silver-fox coats were so common! Annabel defended her taste with the retort that they were not common, either. Midge then said that they were so. She added that everybody had a silver-fox coat. She went on, with perhaps a slight toss of head, to declare that she herself wouldn't be caught dead in silver fox.

For the next few days, though the girls saw each other as constantly, their conversation was careful and infrequent, and they did not once play their game. Then one morning, as soon as Annabel entered the office, she came to Midge and said she had changed her mind. She would not buy a silver-fox coat with any part of her million dollars. Immediately on receiving the legacy, she would select a coat of mink.

Midge smiled and her eyes shone. "I think," she said, "you're doing absolutely the right thing."

Now, as they walked along Fifth Avenue, they played the game anew. It was one of those days with which September is repeatedly cursed; hot and glaring, with slivers of dust in the wind. People drooped and shambled, but the girls carried themselves tall and walked a straight line, as befitted young heiresses on their afternoon promenade. There was no longer need for them to start the game at its formal opening. Annabel went direct to the heart of it.

"All right," she said. "So you've got this million

dollars. So what would be the first thing you'd do?"

"Well, the first thing I'd do," Midge said, "I'd get a mink coat." But she said it mechanically, as if she were giving the memorized answer to an expected question.

"Yes," Annabel said. "I think you ought to. The terribly dark kind of mink." But she, too, spoke as if by rote. It was too hot; fur, no matter how dark and sleek and supple, was horrid to the thoughts.

They stepped along in silence for a while. Then Midge's eye was caught by a shop window. Cool, lovely gleamings were there set off by chaste and elegant darkness.

"No," Midge said, "I take it back. I wouldn't get a mink coat the first thing. Know what I'd do? I'd get a string of pearls. Real pearls."

Annabel's eyes turned to follow Midge's.

"Yes," she said, slowly. "I think that's a kind of a good idea. And it would make sense, too. Because you can wear pearls with anything."

Together they went over to the shop window and stood pressed against it. It contained but one object— a double row of great, even pearls clasped by a deep emerald around a little pink velvet throat.

"What do you suppose they cost?" Annabel said.

"Gee, I don't know," Midge said. "Plenty, I guess."

"Like a thousand dollars?" Annabel said.

"Oh, I guess like more," Midge said. "On account of the emerald."

"Well, like ten thousand dollars?" Annabel said.

"Gee, I wouldn't even know," Midge said.

The devil nudged Annabel in the ribs. "Dare you to go in and price them," she said.

"Like fun!" Midge said.

"Dare you," Annabel said.

"Why, a store like this wouldn't even be open this afternoon," Midge said.

"Yes, it is so, too," Annabel said. "People just came out. And there's a doorman on. Dare you."

"Well," Midge said. "But you've got to come too."

They tendered thanks, icily, to the doorman for ushering them into the shop. It was cool and quiet, a broad, gracious room with paneled walls and soft carpet. But the girls wore expressions of bitter disdain, as if they stood in a sty.

A slim, immaculate clerk came to them and bowed. His neat face showed no astonishment at their appearance.

"Good afternoon," he said. He implied that he would never forget it if they would grant him the favor of accepting his soft-spoken greeting.

"Good afternoon," Annabel and Midge said together, and in like freezing accents.

"Is there something—?" the clerk said.

"Oh, we're just looking," Annabel said. It was as if she flung the words down from a dais.

The clerk bowed.

"My friend and myself merely happened to be passing," Midge said, and stopped, seeming to listen to the phrase. "My friend here and myself," she went on, "merely happened to be wondering how much are those pearls you've got in your window."

"Ah, yes," the clerk said. "The double rope. That is two hundred and fifty thousand dollars, Madam."

"I see," Midge said.

The clerk bowed. "An exceptionally beautiful necklace," he said. "Would you care to look at it?"

"No, thank you," Annabel said.

"My friend and myself merely happened to be passing," Midge said.

They turned to go; to go, from their manner, where the tumbrel awaited them. The clerk sprang ahead and opened the door. He bowed as they swept by him.

The girls went on along the Avenue and disdain was still on their faces.

"Honestly!" Annabel said. "Can you imagine a thing like that?"

"Two hundred and fifty thousand dollars!" Midge

said. "That's a quarter of a million dollars right there!"

"He's got his nerve!" Annabel said.

They walked on. Slowly the disdain went, slowly and completely as if drained from them, and with it went the regal carriage and tread. Their shoulders dropped and they dragged their feet; they bumped against each other, without notice or apology, and caromed away again. They were silent and their eyes were cloudy.

Suddenly Midge straightened her back, flung her head high, and spoke, clear and strong.

"Listen, Annabel," she said. "Look. Suppose there was this terribly rich person, see? You don't know this person, but this person has seen you somewhere and wants to do something for you. Well, it's a terribly old person, see? And so this person dies, just like going to sleep, and leaves you ten million dollars. Now, what would be the first thing you'd do?"

The Oval Portrait

BY EDGAR ALLAN POE

The chateau in which my valet had ventured to make forcible entrance, rather than permit me, in my desperately wounded condition, to pass a night in the open air, was one of those piles of commingled gloom and grandeur which have so long frowned among the Apennines, not less in fact than in the fancy of Mrs. Radcliffe. To all appearance it had been temporarily and very lately abandoned. We established ourselves in one of the smallest and least sumptuously furnished apartments. It lay in a remote turret of the building. Its decorations were rich, yet tattered and antique. Its walls were hung with tapestry and bedecked with manifold and multiform armorial trophies, together with an unusually great number of very spirited modern paintings in frames of rich golden arabesque. In these paintings, which depended from the walls not only in their main surfaces, but in very many nooks which the bizarre architecture of the chateau rendered necessary—in these paintings my incipient delirium, perhaps, had caused me to take deep interest; so that I bade Pedro to close the heavy shutters of the room, since it was already night, to light the tongues of a tall candelabrum which stood by the head of the bed, and to throw open far and wide the fringed curtains of black velvet which enveloped the bed itself. I wished all this done that I might resign myself, if not to sleep, at least alternately to the contemplation of these pictures, and the perusal of a small volume which had been found upon the pillow, and which purported to criticize and explain them.

Long, long I read—and devoutly, devotedly I gazed. Rapidly and gloriously the hours flew by and the deep midnight came. The position of the candelabrum displeased me, and outreaching my hand with difficulty, rather than disturb my slumbering valet, I placed it so as to throw its rays more fully upon the book.

But the action produced an effect altogether unanticipated. The rays of the numerous candles (for there were many) now fell within a niche of the room which had hitherto been thrown into deep shade by one of the bed-posts. I thus saw in vivid light a picture all unnoticed before. It was the portrait of a young girl just ripening into womanhood. I glanced at the painting hurriedly, and then closed my eyes. Why I did this was not at first apparent even to my own perception. But while my lids remained thus shut, I ran over in my mind my reason for so shutting them. It was an impulsive movement to gain time for thought, to make sure that my vision had not deceived me, to calm and subdue my fancy for a more sober and more certain gaze. In a very few moments I again looked fixedly at the painting.

That I now saw aright I could not and would not doubt; for the first flashing of the candles upon that canvas had seemed to dissipate the dreamy stupor which was stealing over my senses, and to startle me at once into waking life.

The portrait, as I have already said, was that of a young girl. It was a mere head and shoulders, done in what is technically termed a vignette manner, much in the style of the favorite heads of Sully. The arms, the bosom, and even the ends of the radiant hair melted imperceptibly into the vague yet deep shadow which formed the background of the whole. The frame was oval, richly gilded and filagreed in Moresque. As a thing of art nothing could be more admirable than the painting itself. But it could have been neither the execution of the work, nor the immortal beauty of the countenance, which had so suddenly and so vehemently moved me. Least of all, could it have been that my fancy, shaken from its half slumber, had mistaken the head for that of a living person. I saw at once that the peculiarities of the design, of the vignetting, and of the frame, must have instantly dispelled such idea— must have prevented even its momentary entertainment. Thinking earnestly upon these points, I remained, for an hour perhaps, half sitting, half reclining, with my vision riveted upon the portrait. At length, satisfied with the true secret of its effect, I fell back within the bed. I had found the spell of the picture in an absolute *life-likeness* of expression, which, at first startling, finally confounded, subdued, and appalled me. With deep and reverent awe I replaced the candelabrum in its former position. The cause of my deep agitation being thus shut from view, I sought eagerly the volume which discussed the paintings and their histories. Turning to the number which designated the oval portrait, I there read the vague and quaint words which follow:

She was a maiden of rarest beauty, and not more lovely than full of glee. And evil was the hour when she saw, and loved, and wedded the painter. He, passionate, studious, austere, and having already a bride in his Art: she a maiden of rarest beauty, and not more lovely than full of glee; all light and smiles, and frolicsome as the young fawn; loving and cherishing all things; hating only the Art which was her rival; dreading only the palette and brushes and other untoward instruments which deprived her of the countenance of her lover. It was thus a terrible thing for this lady to hear the painter speak of his desire to portray even his young bride. But she was humble and obedient, and sat meekly for many weeks in the dark high turret-chamber where the light dripped upon the pale canvas only from overhead. But he, the painter, took glory in his work, which went on from hour to hour, and from day to day. And he was a passionate and wild, and moody man, who became lost in reveries; so that he *would* not see the light which fell so ghastly in that lone turret withered the health and the spirits of his bride, who pined visibly to all but him. Yet she smiled on and still on, uncomplainingly, because she saw that the painter (who had high renown) took a fervid and burning pleasure in his task, and wrought day and night to depict her who so loved him, yet who grew daily more dispirited and weak. And in sooth some who beheld the portrait spoke of its resemblance in low words, as of a mighty marvel, and a proof not less of the power of the painter than of his deep love for her whom he depicted so surpassingly well. But at length, as the labor drew nearer to its conclusion, there were admitted none into the turret; for the painter had grown wild with the ardor of his work, and turned his eyes from the canvas rarely, even to regard the countenance of his wife. And he *would* not see that the tints which he spread upon the canvas were drawn from the cheeks of her who sat beside him. And when many weeks had passed, and but little remained to do, save one brush upon the mouth and one tint upon the eye, the spirit of the lady again flickered up as the flame within the socket of the lamp. And then the brush was given, and then the tint was placed; and for one moment, the painter stood entranced before the work which he had wrought; but in the next, while he yet gazed, he grew tremulous and very pallid, and aghast, and crying with a loud voice, "This is indeed *Life* itself!" turned suddenly to regard his beloved—*She was dead.*

Three Letters . . . and a Footnote

BY HORACIO QUIROGA

Sir:

I am taking the liberty of sending you these lines, hoping you will be good enough to publish them under your own name. I make this request of you because I am informed that no newspaper would accept these pages if I sign them myself. If you think it wiser, you may alter my impressions by giving them a few masculine touches, which indeed may improve them.

My work makes it necessary for me to take the streetcar twice a day, and for five years I have been making the same trip. Sometimes, on the return ride, I travel in the company of some of my girl friends, but on the way to work I always go alone. I am twenty years old, tall, not too thin, and not at all dark-complexioned. My mouth is somewhat large but not pale. My impression is that my eyes are not small. These outward features which I've estimated modestly, as you have observed, are nevertheless all I need to help me form an opinion of many men, in fact so many that I'm tempted to say all men.

You know also that you men have the habit before you board a streetcar of looking rapidly at its occupants through the windows. In that way you examine all the faces (of the women, of course, since they are the only ones that have any interest for you). After that little ceremony, you enter and sit down.

Very well then; as soon as a man leaves the sidewalk, walks over to the car and looks inside, I know perfectly what sort of fellow he is, and I never make a mistake. I know if he is serious, or if he merely intends to invest ten cents of his fare in finding an easy pick-up. I quickly distinguish between those who like to ride at their ease, and those who prefer less room at the side of some girl.

When the place beside me is unoccupied, I recognize accurately, according to the glance through the window, which men are indifferent and will sit down anywhere, which are only half-interested and will turn their heads in order to give us the once-over slowly, after they have sat down; and finally, which are the enterprising fellows who will pass by seven empty places so as to perch uncomfortably at my side, way back in the rear of the vehicle.

Presumably, these fellows are the most interesting. Quite contrary to the regular habit of girls who travel alone, instead of getting up and offering the inside place to the newcomer, I simply move over toward the window to leave plenty of room for the enterprising arrival.

Plenty of room. That's a meaningless phrase. Never will the three quarters of a bench abandoned by a girl to her neighbor be sufficient. After moving and shifting at will, he seems suddenly overcome by a surprising motionlessness, to the point where he seems paralyzed. But that is mere appearance, for if anyone watches with suspicion this lack of movement, he will note that the body of the gentleman, imperceptibly, and with a slyness that does honor to his absent-minded look, is slipping little by little down an imaginary inclined plane toward the window, where the girl happens to be, although he isn't looking at her and apparently has no interest in her at all.

That's the way such men are: one could swear that they're thinking about the moon. However, all this time, the right foot (or the left) continues slipping delicately down the aforementioned plane.

I'll admit that while this is going on, I'm very far from being bored. With a mere glance as I shift toward the window, I have taken the measure of my gallant. I know whether he is a spirited fellow who yields to his first impulse or whether he is really someone brazen enough to give me cause for a little worry. I know whether he is a courteous young man or just a vulgar one, whether a hardened criminal or a tender pickpocket, whether he is really a seductive Beau Brummel (the *seduisant* and not the *seducteur* of the French) or a mere petty masher.

At first view it might seem that only one kind of man would perform the act of letting his foot slip slyly over while his face wears a hypocritical mask, namely the thief. However that is not so, and there isn't a girl that hasn't made this observation. For each different type she must have ready a special defense. But very often, especially if the man is quite young or poorly dressed, he is likely to be a pickpocket.

The tactics followed by the man never vary. First of all the sudden rigidity and the air of thinking about the moon. The next step is a fleeting glimpse at our person which seems to linger slightly over our face, but whose sole purpose is to estimate the distance that intervenes between his foot and ours. This information acquired, now the conquest begins.

I think there are few things funnier than that maneuver you men execute, when you move your foot along in gradual shifts of toe and heel alternately. Obviously you men can't see the joke; but this pretty cat and mouse game played with a size eleven shoe at one end, and at the other, up above, near the roof, a simpering idiotic face (doubtless because of emotion), bears no comparison so far as absurdity is concerned with anything else you men do.

I said before that I was not bored with these performances. And my entertainment is based upon the following fact: from the moment the charmer has calculated with perfect precision the distance he has to cover with his foot, he rarely lets his gaze wander down again. He is certain of his measurement and he has no desire to put us on our guard by repeated glances. You will clearly realize that the attraction for him lies in making contact, and not in merely looking.

Very well then: when this amiable neighbor has gone about halfway, I start the same maneuver that he is executing, and I do it with equal slyness and the same semblance of absent-minded preoccupation with, let us say, my doll. Only, the movement of my foot is away from his. Not much; a few inches are enough.

It's a treat to behold, presently, my neighbor's surprise when, upon arriving finally at the calculated spot, he contacts absolutely nothing. Nothing! His size eleven shoe is entirely alone. This is too much for him; first he takes a look at the floor, and then at my face. My thought is still wandering a thousand leagues away, playing with my doll; but the fellow begins to understand.

Fifteen out of seventeen times (I mention these figures after long experience) the annoying gentleman gives up the enterprise. In the two remaining cases I am forced to resort to a warning look. It isn't necessary for this look to indicate by its expression a feeling of insult, or contempt, or anger: it is enough to make a movement of the head in his direction, toward him but without looking straight at him. In these cases it is better always to avoid crossing glances with a man who by chance has been really and deeply attracted to us. There may be in any pickpocket the makings of a dangerous thief. This fact is well known to the cashiers who guard large amounts of money and also to young women, not thin, not dark, with mouths not little and eyes not small, as is the case with yours truly,

                              M.R.

Dear Miss:
    Deeply grateful for your kindness. I'll sign my name with much pleasure to the article on your impressions,

as you request. Nevertheless, it would interest me very much and purely as your collaborator to know your answer to the following questions: Aside from the seventeen concrete cases you mention, haven't you ever felt the slightest attraction toward some neighbor, tall or short, blond or dark, stout or lean? Haven't you ever felt the vaguest temptation to yield, ever so vague, which made the withdrawing of your own foot disagreeable and troublesome?

H.Q.

Sir:

To be frank, yes, once in my life, I felt that temptation to yield to someone, or more accurately, that lack of energy in my foot to which you refer. That person was *you*. But you didn't have the sense to take advantage of it.

M.R.

An Attempt at Reform

BY AUGUST STRINDBERG

She had noticed with indignation that girls were solely brought up to be housekeepers for their future husbands. Therefore she had learned a trade which would enable her to keep herself in all circumstances of life. She made artificial flowers.

He had noticed with regret that girls simply waited for a husband who should keep them; he resolved to marry a free and independent woman who could earn her own living; such a woman would be his equal and a companion for life, not a housekeeper.

Fate ordained that they should meet. He was an artist and she made, as I already mentioned, flowers; they were both living in Paris at the time when they conceived these ideas.

There was style in their marriage. They took three rooms at Passy. In the centre was the studio, to the right of it his room, to the left hers. This did away with the common bedroom and double bed, that abomination which has no counterpart in nature and is responsible for a great deal of dissipation and immorality. It moreover did away with the inconvenience of having to dress and undress in the same room. It was far better that each of them should have a separate room and that the studio should be a neutral, common meeting-place.

They required no servant; they were going to do the cooking themselves and employ an old charwoman in the mornings and evenings. It was all very well thought out and excellent in theory.

"But supposing you had children?" asked the sceptics.

"Nonsense, there won't be any!"

It worked splendidly. He went to the market in the morning and did the catering. Then he made the coffee. She made the beds and put the rooms in order. And then they sat down and worked.

When they were tired of working they gossiped, gave one another good advice, laughed and were very jolly.

At twelve o'clock he lit the kitchen fire and she prepared the vegetables. He cooked the beef, while she ran across the street to the grocer's; then she laid the table and he dished up the dinner.

Of course, they loved one another as husbands and wives do. They said good night to each other and went into their own rooms, but there was no lock to keep him out when he knocked at her door; but the accommodation was small and the morning found them in their own quarters. Then he knocked at the wall.

"Good morning, little girlie, how are you today?"

"Very well, darling, and you?"

Their meeting at breakfast was always like a new experience which never grew stale.

They often went out together in the evening and frequently met their countrymen. She had no objection to the smell of tobacco, and was never in the way. Everybody said it was an ideal marriage; no one had ever known a happier couple.

But the young wife's parents, who lived a long way off, were always writing and asking all sorts of indelicate questions; they were longing to have a grandchild. Louisa ought to remember that the institution of marriage existed for the benefit of the children, not the parents. Louisa held that this view was an old-fashioned one. Mama asked whether she did not think that the result of the new ideas would be the complete extirpation of mankind? Louisa had never looked at it in that light, and moreover the question did not interest her. Both she and her husband were happy;

at last the spectacle of a happy married couple was presented to the world, and the world was envious.

Life was very pleasant. Neither of them was master and they shared expenses. Now he earned more, now she did, but in the end their contributions to the common fund amounted to the same figure.

Then she had a birthday! She was awakened in the morning by the entrance of the charwoman with a bunch of flowers and a letter painted all over with flowers, and containing the following words:

"To the lady flower-bud from her dauber, who wishes her many happy returns of the day and begs her to honor him with her company at an excellent little breakfast—at once."

She knocked at his door—come in!

And they breakfasted, sitting on the bed—his bed; and the charwoman was kept the whole day to do all the work. It was a lovely birthday!

Their happiness never palled. It lasted two years. All the prophets had prophesied falsely.

It was a model marriage!

But when two years had passed, the young wife fell ill. She put it down to some poison contained in the wall-paper; he suggested germs of some sort. Yes, certainly, germs. But something was wrong. Something was not as it should be. She must have caught cold. Then she grew stout. Was she suffering from tumour? Yes, they were afraid that she was.

She consulted a doctor—and came home crying. It was indeed a growth, but one which would one day see daylight, grow into a flower and bear fruit.

The husband did anything but cry. He found style in it, and then the wretch went to his club and boasted about it to his friends. But the wife still wept. What would her position be now? She would soon not be able to earn money with her work and then she would have to live on him. And they would have to have a servant! Ugh! those servants!

All their care, their caution, their wariness had been wrecked on the rock of the inevitable.

But the mother-in-law wrote enthusiastic letters and repeated over and over again that marriage was instituted by God for the protection of the children; the parents' pleasure counted for very little.

Hugo implored her to forget the fact that she would not be able to earn anything in future. Didn't she do her full share of the work by mothering the baby? Wasn't that as good as money? Money was, rightly understood, nothing but work. Therefore she paid her share in full.

It took her a long time to get over the fact that he had to keep her. But when the baby came, she forgot all about it. She remained his wife and companion as before in addition to being the mother of his child, and he found that this was worth more than anything else.

The Three Hermits

AN OLD LEGEND CURRENT IN
THE VOLGA DISTRICT

BY LEO TOLSTOY

"And in praying use not vain repetitions as the Gentiles do: for they think that they shall be heard for their much speaking. Be not therefore like them: for your Father knoweth what things ye have need of, before ye ask Him."

Matthew vi:7,8.

A Bishop was sailing from Archangel to the Solovétsk Monastery, and on the same vessel were a number of pilgrims on their way to visit the shrines at that place. The voyage was a smooth one. The wind favorable and the weather fair. The pilgrims lay on deck, eating, or sat in groups talking to one another. The Bishop, too, came on deck, and as he was pacing up and down he noticed a group of men standing near the prow and listening to a fisherman, who was pointing to the sea and telling them something. The Bishop stopped, and looked in the direction in which the man was pointing. He could see nothing, however, but the sea glistening in the sunshine. He drew nearer to listen, but when the man saw him, he took off his cap and was silent. The rest of the people also took off their caps and bowed.

"Do not let me disturb you, friends," said the Bishop. "I came to hear what this good man was saying."

"The fisherman was telling us about the hermits,"

replied one, a tradesman, rather bolder than the rest.

"What hermits?" asked the Bishop, going to the side of the vessel and seating himself on a box. "Tell me about them. I should like to hear. What were you pointing at?"

"Why, that little island you can just see over there," answered the man, pointing to a spot ahead and a little to the right. "That is the island where the hermits live for the salvation of their souls."

"Where is the island?" asked the Bishop. "I see nothing."

"There, in the distance, if you will please look along my hand. Do you see that little cloud? Below it, and a bit to the left, there is just a faint streak. That is the island."

The Bishop looked carefully, but his unaccustomed eyes could make out nothing but the water shimmering in the sun.

"I cannot see it," he said. "But who are the hermits that live there?"

"They are holy men," answered the fisherman. "I had long heard tell of them, but never chanced to see them myself till the year before last."

And the fisherman related how once, when he was out fishing, he had been stranded at night upon that island, not knowing where he was. In the morning, as he wandered about the island, he came across an earth hut, and met an old man standing near it. Presently two others came out, and after having fed him and dried his things, they helped him mend his boat.

"And what are they like?" asked the Bishop.

"One is a small man and his back is bent. He wears a priest's cassock and is very old; he must be more than a hundred, I should say. He is so old that the white of his beard is taking a greenish tinge, but he is always smiling, and his face is as bright as an angel's from heaven. The second is taller, but he also is very old. He wears a tattered peasant coat. His beard is broad, and of a yellowish grey color. He is a strong man. Before I had time to help him, he turned my boat over as if it were only a pail. He too is kindly and cheerful. The third is tall, and has a beard as white as snow and reaching to his knees. He is stern, with overhanging eyebrows; and he wears nothing but a piece of matting tied round his waist."

"And did they speak to you?" asked the Bishop.

"For the most part they did everything in silence, and spoke but little even to one another. One of them would just give a glance, and the others would understand him. I asked the tallest whether they had lived there long. He frowned, and muttered something as if he were angry; but the oldest one took his hand and smiled, and then the tall one was quiet. The oldest one only said: 'Have mercy upon us,' and smiled."

While the fisherman was talking, the ship had drawn nearer to the island.

"There, now you can see it plainly, if your Lordship will please to look," said the tradesman, pointing with his hand.

The Bishop looked, and now he really saw a dark streak—which was the island. Having looked at it a while, he left the prow of the vessel, and going to the stern, asked the helmsman:

"What island is that?"

"That one," replied the man, "has no name. There are many such in this sea."

"Is it true that there are hermits who live there for the salvation of their souls?"

"So it is said, your Lordship, but I don't know if it's true. Fishermen say they have seen them; but of course they may only be spinning yarns."

"I should like to land on the island and see these men," said the Bishop. "How could I manage it?"

"The ship cannot get close to the island," replied the helmsman, "but you might be rowed there in a boat. You had better speak to the captain."

The captain was sent for and came.

"I should like to see these hermits," said the Bishop. "Could I not be rowed ashore?"

The captain tried to dissuade him.

"Of course it could be done," said he, "but we should lose much time. And if I might venture to say so to your Lordship, the old men are not worth your pains. I have heard say that they are foolish old fellows, who understand nothing, and never speak a word, any more than the fish in the sea."

"I wish to see them," said the Bishop, "and I will pay you for your trouble and loss of time. Please let me have a boat."

There was no help for it; so the order was given. The sailors trimmed the sails, the steersman put up the helm, and the ship's course was set for the island. A chair was placed at the prow for the Bishop, and he sat there, looking ahead. The passengers all collected at the prow, and gazed at the island. Those who had the sharpest eyes could presently make out the rocks on it, and then a mud hut was seen. At last one man saw the hermits themselves. The captain brought a telescope and, after looking through it, handed it to the Bishop.

"It's right enough. There are three men standing on the shore. There, a little to the right of that big rock."

The Bishop took the telescope, got it into position, and he saw the three men: a tall one, a shorter one, and one very small and bent, standing on the shore and holding each other by the hand.

The captain turned to the Bishop.

"The vessel can get no nearer in than this, your Lordship. If you wish to go ashore, we must ask you to go in the boat, while we anchor here."

The cable was quickly let out; the anchor cast, and the sails furled. There was a jerk, and the vessel shook. Then, a boat having been lowered, the oarsmen jumped in, and the Bishop descended the ladder and took his seat. The men pulled at their oars and the boat moved rapidly towards the island. When they came within a stone's throw, they saw three old men: a tall one with only a piece of matting tied round his waist: a shorter one in a tattered peasant coat, and a very old one bent with age and wearing an old cassock—all three standing hand in hand.

The oarsmen pulled in to the shore, and held on with the boathook while the Bishop got out.

The old men bowed to him, and he gave them his blessing, at which they bowed still lower. Then the Bishop began to speak to them.

"I have heard," he said, "that you, godly men, live here saving your own souls and praying to our Lord Christ for your fellow men. I, an unworthy servant of Christ, am called, by God's mercy, to keep and teach His flock. I wished to see you, servants of God, and to do what I can to teach you, also."

The old men looked at each other smiling, but remained silent.

"Tell me," said the Bishop, "what you are doing to save your souls, and how you serve God on this island."

The second hermit sighed, and looked at the oldest, the very ancient one. The latter smiled, and said:

"We do not know how to serve God. We only serve and support ourselves, servant of God."

"But how do you pray to God?" asked the Bishop.

"We pray in this way," replied the hermit. "Three are ye, three are we, have mercy upon us."

And when the old man said this, all three raised their eyes to heaven, and repeated:

"Three are ye, three are we, have mercy upon us!"

The Bishop smiled.

"You have evidently heard something about the Holy Trinity," said he. "But you do not pray aright. You have won my affection, godly men. I see you wish to please the Lord, but you do not know how to serve Him. That is not the way to pray; but listen to me, and I will teach you. I will teach you, not a way of my own, but the way in which God in the Holy Scriptures has commanded all men to pray to Him."

And the Bishop began explaining to the hermits how God had revealed Himself to men; telling them of God the Father, and God the Son, and God the Holy Ghost.

"God the Son came down on earth," said he, "to save men, and this is how He taught us all to pray. Listen, and repeat after me: 'Our Father.'"

And the first old man repeated after him, "Our Father," and the second said, "Our Father," and the third said, "Our Father."

"Which art in heaven," continued the Bishop.

The first hermit repeated, "Which art in heaven," but the second blundered over the words, and the tall hermit could not say them properly. His hair had grown over his mouth so that he could not speak plainly. The very old hermit, having no teeth, also mumbled indistinctly.

The Bishop repeated the words again, and the old men repeated them after him. The Bishop sat down on a stone, and the old men stood before him, watching his mouth, and repeating the words as he uttered them. And all day long the Bishop labored, saying a word twenty, thirty, a hundred times over, and the old men repeated it after him. They blundered, and he corrected them, and made them begin again.

The Bishop did not leave off till he had taught them the whole of the Lord's Prayer so that they could not only repeat it after him, but could say it by themselves. The middle one was the first to know it, and to repeat the whole of it alone. The Bishop made him say it again and again, and at last the others could say it too.

It was getting dark and the moon was appearing over the water, before the Bishop rose to return to the vessel. When he took leave of the old men they all bowed down to the ground before him. He raised them, and kissed each of them, telling them to pray as he had taught them. Then he got into the boat and returned to the ship.

And as he sat in the boat and was rowed to the ship he could hear the three voices of the hermits loudly repeating the Lord's Prayer. As the boat drew near the vessel their voices could no longer be heard, but they could still be seen in the moonlight, standing as he had left them on the shore, the shortest in the middle, the tallest on the right, the middle one on the left. As soon as the Bishop had reached the vessel and got on board, the anchor was weighed and the sails unfurled. The wind filled them and the ship sailed away, and the Bishop took a seat in the stern and watched the island they had left. For a time he could still see the hermits, but presently they disappeared from sight, though the island was still visible. At last it too vanished, and only the sea was to be seen, rippling in the moonlight.

The pilgrims lay down to sleep, and all was quiet on deck. The Bishop did not wish to sleep, but sat alone at the stern, gazing at the sea where the island was no longer visible, and thinking of the good old men. He thought how pleased they had been to learn the Lord's Prayer; and he thanked God for having sent him to teach and help such godly men.

So the Bishop sat, thinking, and gazing at the sea where the island had disappeared. And the moonlight flickered before his eyes, sparkling, now here, now there, upon the waves. Suddenly he saw something white and shining, on the bright path which the moon cast across the sea. Was it a seagull, or the little gleaming sail of some small boat? The Bishop fixed his eyes on it, wondering.

"It must be a boat sailing after us," thought he, "but it is overtaking us very rapidly. It was far, far away a minute ago, but now it is much nearer. It cannot be a boat, for I can see no sail; but whatever it may be, it is following us and catching us up."

And he could not make out what it was. Not a boat, nor a bird, nor a fish! It was too large for a man, and besides a man could not be out there in the midst of the sea. The Bishop rose, and said to the helmsman:

"Look there, what is that, my friend? What is it?" the Bishop repeated, though he could now see plainly what it was—the three hermits running upon the water, all gleaming white, their grey beards shining, and approaching the ship as quickly as though it were not moving.

The steersman looked, and let go the helm in terror.

"Oh, Lord! The hermits are running after us on the water as though it were dry land!"

The passengers, hearing him, jumped up and crowded to the stern. They saw the hermits coming along hand in hand, and the two outer ones beckoning the ship to stop. All three were gliding along upon the water without moving their feet. Before the ship could be stopped, the hermits had reached it, and raising their heads, all three as with one voice, began to say:

"We have forgotten your teaching, servant of God. As long as we kept repeating it we remembered, but when we stopped saying it for a time, a word dropped out, and now it has all gone to pieces. We can remember nothing of it. Teach us again."

The Bishop crossed himself, and leaning over the ship's side, said:

"Your own prayer will reach the Lord, men of God. It is not for me to teach you. Pray for us sinners."

And the Bishop bowed low before the old men; and they turned and went back across the sea. And a light shone until daybreak on the spot where they were lost to sight.

The Phœnix

BY SYLVIA TOWNSEND WARNER

▱ ▱ ▱

Lord Strawberry, a nobleman, collected birds. He had the finest aviary in Europe, so large that eagles did not find it uncomfortable, so well laid out that both humming-birds and snow-buntings had a climate that suited them perfectly. But for many years the finest set of apartments remained empty, with just a label saying: "PHŒNIX. *Habitat: Arabia.*"

Many authorities on bird life had assured Lord Strawberry that the phœnix is a fabulous bird, or that the breed was long extinct. Lord Strawberry was unconvinced: his family had always believed in phœnixes. At intervals he received from his agents (together with statements of their expenses) birds which they declared were the phœnix but which turned out to be orioles, macaws, turkey buzzards dyed orange, etc. or stuffed cross-breeds, ingeniously assembled from various plumages. Finally Lord Strawberry went himself to Arabia, where, after some months, he found a phœnix, won its confidence, caught it, and brought it home in perfect condition.

It was a remarkably fine phœnix, with a charming character—affable to the other birds in the aviary and much attached to Lord Strawberry. On its arrival in England it made a great stir among ornithologists, journalists, poets, and milliners, and was constantly visited. But it was not puffed by these attentions, and when it was no longer in the news, and the visits fell off, it showed no pique or rancour. It ate well, and seemed perfectly contented.

It costs a great deal of money to keep up an aviary. When Lord Strawberry died he died penniless. The aviary came on the market. In normal times the rarer birds, and certainly the phœnix, would have been bid for by the trustees of Europe's great zoological societies, or by private persons in the U.S.A.; but as it happened Lord Strawberry died just after a world war, when both money and bird-seed were hard to come by (indeed the cost of bird-seed was one of the things which had ruined Lord Strawberry). The London *Times* urged in a leader that the phœnix be bought for the London Zoo, saying that a nation of bird-lovers had a moral right to own such a rarity and a fund, called the Strawberry Phœnix Fund, was opened. Students, naturalists, and school-children contributed according to their means; but their means were small, and there were no large donations. So Lord Strawberry's executors (who had the death duties to consider) closed with the higher offer of Mr. Tancred Poldero, owner and proprietor of Poldero's Wizard Wonderworld.

For quite a while Mr. Poldero considered his phœnix a bargain. It was a civil and obliging bird, and adapted itself readily to its new surroundings. It did not cost much to feed, it did not mind children; and though it had no tricks, Mr. Poldero supposed it would soon pick up some. The publicity of the Strawberry Phœnix Fund was now most helpful. Almost every contributor now saved up another half-crown in order to see the phœnix. Others, who had not contributed to the fund, even paid double to look at it on the five-shilling days.

But then business slackened. The phœnix was as handsome as ever, and as amiable; but, as Mr. Poldero said, it hadn't got Udge. Even at popular prices the phœnix was not really popular. It was too quiet, too classical. So people went instead to watch the antics of the baboons, or to admire the crocodile who had eaten the woman.

One day Mr. Poldero said to his manager, Mr. Ramkin:

"How long since any fool paid to look at the phœnix?"

"Matter of three weeks," replied Mr. Ramkin.

"Eating his head off," said Mr. Poldero. "Let alone the insurance. Seven shillings a week it costs me to insure that bird, and I might as well insure the Archbishop of Canterbury."

"The public don't like him. He's too quiet for them, that's the trouble. Won't mate nor nothing. And I've tried him with no end of pretty pollies, ospreys, and Cochin-Chinas, and the Lord knows what. But he won't look at them."

"Wonder if we could swap him for a livelier one," said Mr. Poldero.

"Impossible. There's only one of him at a time."

"Go on!"

"I mean it. Haven't you ever read what it says on the label?"

They went to the phœnix's cage. It flapped its wings politely, but they paid no attention. They read:

"PANSY. *Phœnix phœnixissima formosissima arabiana.* This rare and fabulous bird is UNIQUE. The World's Old Bachelor. Has no mate and doesn't want one. When old, sets fire to itself and emerges miraculously reborn. Specially imported from the East."

"I've got an idea," said Mr. Poldero. "How old do you suppose that bird is?"

"Looks in its prime to me," said Mr. Ramkin.

"Suppose," continued Mr. Poldero, "we could somehow get him alight? We'd advertise it beforehand, of course, work up interest. Then we'd have a new bird, and a bird with some romance about it, a bird with a life-story. We could sell a bird like that."

Mr. Ramkin nodded.

"I've read about it in a book," he said. "You've got to give them scented woods and what not, and they build a nest and sit down on it and catch fire spontaneous. But they won't do it till they're old. That's the snag."

"Leave that to me," said Mr. Poldero. "You get those scented woods, and I'll do the ageing."

It was not easy to age the phœnix. Its allowance of food was halved, and halved again, but though it grew thinner its eyes were undimmed and its plumage glossy as ever. The heating was turned off; but it puffed out its feathers against the cold, and seemed none the worse. Other birds were put into its cage, birds of a peevish and quarrelsome nature. They pecked and chivied it; but the phœnix was so civil and amiable that after a day or two they lost their animosity. Then Mr. Poldero tried alley cats. These could not be won by manners, but the phœnix darted above their heads and flapped its golden wings in their faces, and daunted them.

Mr. Poldero turned to a book on Arabia, and read that the climate was dry. "Aha!" said he. The phœnix was moved to a small cage that had a sprinkler in the ceiling. Every night the sprinkler was turned on. The phœnix began to cough. Mr. Poldero had another good idea. Daily he stationed himself in front of the cage to jeer at the bird and abuse it.

When spring was come, Mr. Poldero felt justified in beginning a publicity campaign about the ageing phœnix. The old public favourite, he said, was nearing its end. Meanwhile he tested the bird's reactions every few days by putting a few tufts of foul-smelling straw and some strands of rusty barbed wire into the cage, to see if it were interested in nesting yet. One day the phœnix began turning over the straw. Mr. Poldero signed a contract for the film rights. At last the hour seemed ripe. It was a fine Saturday evening in May. For some weeks the public interest in the ageing phœnix had been working up, and the admission charge had risen to five shillings. The enclosure was thronged. The lights and the cameras were trained on the cage, and a loud-speaker proclaimed to the audience the rarity of what was about to take place.

"The phœnix," said the loud-speaker, "is the aristocrat of bird-life. Only the rarest and most expensive specimens of oriental wood, drenched in exotic perfumes, will tempt him to construct his strange love-nest."

Now a neat assortment of twigs and shavings, strongly scented, was shoved into the cage.

"The phœnix," the loud-speaker continued, "is as capricious as Cleopatra, as luxurious as la du Barry, as heady as a strain of wild gypsy music. All the fantastic pomp and passion of the ancient East, its languorous magic, its subtle cruelties . . ."

"Lawks!" cried a woman in the crowd. "He's at it!"

A quiver stirred the dulled plumage. The phœnix turned its head from side to side. It descended, staggering, from its perch. Then wearily it began to pull about the twigs and shavings.

The cameras clicked, the lights blazed full on the cage. Rushing to the loud-speaker Mr. Poldero exclaimed:

"Ladies and gentlemen, this is the thrilling moment the world has breathlessly awaited. The legend of centuries is materializing before our modern eyes. The phœnix . . ."

The phœnix settled on its pyre and appeared to fall asleep.

The film director said:

"Well, if it doesn't evaluate more than this, mark it instructional."

At that moment the phœnix and the pyre burst into flames. The flames streamed upwards, leaped out on every side. In a minute or two everything was burned to ashes, and some thousand people, including Mr. Poldero, perished in the blaze.

The Hour of Letdown

BY E. B. WHITE

▱ ▱ ▱

When the man came in, carrying the machine, most of us looked up from our drinks, because we had never seen anything like it before. The man set the thing down on top of the bar near the beerpulls. It took up an ungodly amount of room and you could see the bartender didn't like it any too well, having this big, ugly-looking gadget parked right there.

"Two rye-and-water," the man said.

The bartender went on puddling an Old-Fashioned that he was working on, but he was obviously turning over the request in his mind.

"You want a double?" he asked, after a bit.

"No," said the man. "Two rye-and-water, please." He stared straight at the bartender, not exactly unfriendly but on the other hand not affirmatively friendly.

Many years of catering to the kind of people that come into saloons had provided the bartender with an adjustable mind. Nevertheless, he did not adjust readily to this fellow, and he did not like the machine—that was sure. He picked up a live cigarette that was idling on the edge of the cash register, took a drag out of it, and returned it thoughtfully. Then he poured two shots of rye whiskey, drew two glasses of water, and shoved the drinks in front of the man. People were watching. When something a little out of the ordinary takes place at a bar, the sense of it spreads quickly all along the line and pulls the customers together.

127

The man gave no sign of being the center of attraction. He laid a five-dollar bill down on the bar. Then he drank one of the ryes and chased it with water. He picked up the other rye, opened a small vent in the machine (it was like an oil cup) and poured the whiskey in, and then poured the water in.

The bartender watched grimly. "Not funny," he said in an even voice. "And furthermore, your companion takes up too much room. Whyn't you put it over on that bench by the door, make more room here."

"There's plenty of room for everyone here," replied the man.

"I ain't amused," said the bartender. "Put the goddam thing over near the door like I say. Nobody will touch it."

The man smiled. "You should have seen it this afternoon," he said. "It was magnificent. Today was the third day of the tournament. Imagine it—three days of continuous brainwork. And against the top players of the country, too. Early in the game it gained an advantage; then for two hours it exploited the advantage brilliantly, ending with the opponent's king backed in a corner. The sudden capture of a knight, the neutralization of a bishop, and it was all over. You know how much money it won, all told, in three days of playing chess?"

"How much?" asked the bartender.

"Five thousand dollars," said the man. "Now it wants to let down, wants to get a little drunk."

The bartender ran his towel vaguely over some wet spots. "Take it somewheres else and get it drunk there!" he said firmly. "I got enough troubles."

The man shook his head and smiled. "No, we like it here." He pointed at the empty glasses. "Do this again, will you, please?"

The bartender slowly shook his head. He seemed dazed but dogged. "You stow the thing away," he ordered. "I'm not ladling out whiskey for jokester-smiths."

" 'Jokesmiths,' " said the machine. "The word is 'jokesmiths.' "

A few feet down the bar, a customer who was on his third highball seemed ready to participate in this conversation to which we had all been listening so attentively. He was a middle-aged man. His necktie was pulled down away from his collar, and he had eased the collar by unbuttoning it. He had pretty nearly finished his third drink, and the alcohol tended to make him throw his support in with the underprivileged and the thirsty.

"If the machine wants another drink, give it another drink," he said to the bartender. "Let's not have haggling."

The fellow with the machine turned to his new-found friend and gravely raised his hand to his temple, giving him a salute of gratitude and fellowship. He addressed his next remark to him, as though deliberately snubbing the bartender.

"You know how it is when you're all fagged out mentally, how you want a drink?"

"Certainly do," replied the friend. "Most natural thing in the world."

There was a stir all along the bar, some seeming to side with the bartender, others with the machine group. A tall, gloomy man standing next to me spoke up.

"Another whiskey sour, Bill," he said. "And go easy on the lemon juice."

"Picric acid," said the machine, sullenly. "They don't use lemon juice in these places."

"That does it!" said the bartender, smacking his hand on the bar. "Will you put that thing away or else beat it out of here. I ain't in the mood, I tell you. I got this saloon to run and I don't want lip from a mechanical brain or whatever the hell you've got there."

The man ignored this ultimatum. He addressed his friend, whose glass was now empty.

"It's not just that it's all tuckered out after three days of chess," he said amiably. "You know another reason it wants a drink?"

"No," said the friend. "Why?"

"It cheated," said the man.

At this remark, the machine chuckled. One of its arms dipped slightly, and a light glowed in a dial.

The friend frowned. He looked as though his dignity had been hurt, as though his trust had been misplaced. "Nobody can cheat at chess," he said. "Simpossible. In chess, everything is open and above the board. The nature of the game of chess is such that cheating is impossible."

"That's what I used to think, too," said the man. "But there *is* a way."

"Well, it doesn't surprise me any," put in the bartender. "The first time I laid my eyes on that crummy thing I spotted it for a crook."

"Two rye-and-water," said the man.

"You can't have the whiskey," said the bartender. He glared at the mechanical brain. "How do I know it ain't drunk already?"

"That's simple. Ask it something," said the man.

The customers shifted and stared into the mirror. We were in this thing now, up to our necks. We waited. It was the bartender's move.

"Ask it what? Such as?" said the bartender.

"Makes no difference. Pick a couple big figures, ask it to multiply them together. You couldn't multiply big figures together if you were drunk, could you?"

The machine shook slightly, as though making internal preparations.

"Ten thousand eight hundred and sixty-two, multiply it by ninety-nine," said the bartender viciously. We could tell that he was throwing in the two nines to make it hard.

The machine flickered. One of its tubes spat, and a hand changed position, jerkily.

"One million seventy-five thousand three hundred and thirty-eight," said the machine.

Not a glass was raised all along the bar. People just stared gloomily into the mirror; some of us studied our own faces, others took carom shots at the man and the machine.

Finally, a youngish, mathematically minded customer got out a piece of paper and a pencil and went into retirement. "It works out," he reported, after some minutes of calculating. "You can't say the machine is drunk!"

Everyone now glared at the bartender. Reluctantly he poured two shots of rye, drew two glasses of water. The man drank his drink. Then he fed the machine its drink. The machine's light grew fainter. One of its cranky little arms wilted.

For a while the saloon simmered along like a ship at sea in calm weather. Every one of us seemed to be trying to digest the situation, with the help of liquor. Quite a few glasses were refilled. Most of us sought help in the mirror—the court of last appeal.

The fellow with the unbuttoned collar settled his score. He walked stiffly over and stood between the man and the machine. He put one arm around the man, the other around the machine. "Let's get out of here and go to a good place," he said.

The machine glowed slightly. It seemed to be a little drunk now.

"All right," said the man. "That suits me fine. I've got my car outside."

He settled for the drinks and put down a tip. Quietly and a trifle uncertainly he tucked the machine under his arm, and he and his companion of the night walked to the door and out into the street.

The bartender stared fixedly, then resumed his light housekeeping. "So he's got his car outside," he said, with heavy sarcasm. "Now isn't that nice!"

A customer at the end of the bar near the door left his drink, stepped to the window, parted the curtains, and looked out. He watched for a moment, then returned to his place and addressed the bartender. "It's even nicer than you think," he said. "It's a Cadillac. And which one of the three of them d'ya think is doing the driving?"

How Grandpa Came into the Money

BY ELSE ZANTNEV

❧ ❧ ❧

He was a sweet soul, my grandfather, but when the brains were passed out he must have been absent. I still marvel how Grandmother could raise a family on his earnings.

We all lived in one little house and we were a scrawny lot. Nobody ever had to coax any of us children to eat. In fact, after having had lunch at my mother's, I would go upstairs to Grandmother and have another one. And then I would visit Aunt Bertha, who lived a few doors away, and eat some more.

What a ripe apple tasted like I found out only when I was well over fifteen and apprenticed to a shopkeeper in the city. Apples did not ripen in our village—they never had a chance. They were so sour they would have pulled the holes in our stockings together. But no apples ever tasted as good again as those little green ones!

One time in my entire childhood I felt good and full: Aunt Bertha had forgotten to lock the larder and I detected, disappeared with, and devoured twenty-two doughnuts. The rest of the family never forgot nor forgave me. Years later when I would arrive at family gatherings someone would always shout, "Watch the doughnuts!"

Perhaps you can imagine what it meant when, one fine day, fortune smiled on Grandfather. He got himself in a trainwreck!

Now, if something like that happened to you (and

you survived) you had it made. The railroad would pay! So all of the lucky passengers knew exactly what to do: they commenced to groan piteously and writhe upon the ground while waiting for the doctors and stretcher bearers to arrive.

All but Grandfather!

He had a better appetite than the rest of us combined. Never in his life had he missed a meal and he was not going to start now. No sir! Not for a puny trainwreck. So he cut himself a stout walking stick and set out for home—a three-hour walk.

In the meantime, the news of the wreck had already reached the village and the telegram had said, "No fatalities."

I cannot describe the many looks that passed across my grandmother's face when she saw her husband come striding in the door, covered with dust, a bit tired from his long walk, but sound of limb and smiling broadly for he was just in time for dinner. First came relief at seeing her man unharmed. Then the relief mingled with and finally was replaced by fury.

Grandfather had passed up his one and only golden opportunity!

So she turned into a kind of tornado. Before he knew what was happening, he found himself minus his pants and in bed. His plaintive protests did him no good. Grandma slapped a wet towel on his head while Mother went to search for the only medicine we had in the house—castor oil!

Grandfather cried out in horror and tried to disappear under the blanket, but Mother clamped his nose shut and dosed him anyway. Poor man! The only thing he really needed was his dinner. But what could he or anyone else do once his wife and daughter had made up their minds.

Having accomplished this much, one of the children was dispatched to get hold of the doctor. He came, gave Grandpa a thorough examination, and was just about to congratulate him on his excellent state of health when my mother went into action.

She planted herself firmly in front of the doctor, drew herself up to her full height of four feet, ten inches, and told him in no uncertain terms, that Grandpa had suffered a severe shock and concussion of whatever brains he had. How else to explain the fact that he walked away from this chance of a lifetime! Did the doctor have another explanation? Ha?

The doctor took one look at her grimly determined face. He had dealt with her before and he knew when he was licked. He resigned himself, accepted my mother's diagnosis, and left.

And then came the time of waiting. The two women did all they could to keep Grandpa in bed and coached him carefully on what to say and what not to say when the railroad people came. Grandpa nodded wisely and promised to cooperate.

But did you ever try to keep an eel in bed? He gave them the slip as often as not. And when, in desperation, they hid his pants, he bribed one of us children to find them for him and got out of bed anyway.

And out of bed he was when we heard the long awaited commotion outside of the house. Peeking through the window we saw the railroad investigators, with the entire village gathered respectfully behind them, waiting to learn the outcome.

Pants, boots and all, Grandpa was stuffed into bed and the covers were pulled up to his chin. The shades were lowered, the bottle of castor oil was placed prominently by his bedside, and the investigators were ushered in.

From the first moment it was clear that Grandpa had forgotten all of the careful coaching. He beamed welcome at the distinguished visitors and complimented them on their good looks. He then went on to talk of the weather and then of the crops. When the railroad doctor finally managed to ask him what injuries he had sustained my mother signalled frantically by pointing to her head.

"Well," said grandfather with an angelic smile, "There's really nothing at all wrong with me that 100,-000 gulden couldn't cure."

Mother promptly fainted. Grandma shrieked and ran from the room. And the claims adjustors doubled up with laughter.

After they had recovered, and revived poor Mama, they awarded Grandpa 5,000 gulden—making him the richest man in the village!

But to his dying day, he could never understand why they had given him the money.

START A COLLECTION

With Bantam's fiction anthologies, you can begin almost anywhere. Choose from science fiction, classic literature, modern short stories, mythology, and more—all by both new and established writers in America and around the world.

☐	THE MARTIAN CHRONICLES Ray Bradbury	5613 •	95¢
☐	THE WORLD'S BEST SHORT STORIES Roger B. Goodman, ed.	6382 •	95¢
☐	75 SHORT MASTERPIECES: Stories from the World's Literature Roger B. Goodman, ed.	6742 •	95¢
☐	MYTHS AND LEGENDS OF ANCIENT EGYPT T. G. H. James	6824 •	$1.45
☐	MYTHS AND LEGENDS OF ANCIENT GREECE John Pinsent	6827 •	$1.45
☐	50 GREAT AMERICAN SHORT STORIES Milton Crane, ed.	6893 •	$1.50
☐	THE ALEPH AND OTHER STORIES, 1939-1969 Jorge Luis Borges	7117 •	$1.95
☐	THE NICK ADAMS STORIES Ernest Hemingway	7250 •	$1.75
☐	TEN TIMES BLACK: Stories from the Black Experience Julian Mayfield, ed.	7351 •	95¢
☐	50 GREAT HORROR STORIES John Canning, ed.	7601 •	$1.50
☐	50 GREAT SHORT STORIES Milton Crane, ed.	8192 •	$1.50
☐	WE BE WORD SORCERERS Sonia Sanchez, ed.	8347 •	$1.25
☐	TEN MODERN AMERICAN SHORT STORIES David A. Sohn, ed.	8571 •	95¢
☐	THE BALLAD OF THE SAD CAFE AND OTHER STORIES Carson McCullers	8596 •	$1.25
☐	TWENTY GRAND SHORT STORIES Ernestine Taggard, ed.	8609 •	95¢

Bantam Book Catalog

It lists over a thousand money-saving best-sellers originally priced from $3.75 to $15.00 —bestsellers that are yours now for as little as 50¢ to $2.95!

The catalog gives you a great opportunity to build your own private library at huge savings!

So don't delay any longer—send us your name and address and 10¢ (to help defray postage and handling costs).